Resisting the Hero

Resisting the Hero

CINDI
MADSEN

Entangled Publishing, LLC
2614 South Timberline Road
Suite 105, PMB 159
Fort Collins, CO 80525
rights@entangledpublishing.com

Bliss is an imprint of Entangled Publishing, LLC.

Edited by Stacy Abrams and Alycia Tornetta
Cover design by Bree Archer
Cover photography by BraunS/iStock

Manufactured in the United States of America

First Edition January 2014

Bliss
an Entangled imprint

To all the heroes out there serving our country and keeping our cities safe, and the people who love and support them.

Chapter One

The bar was bursting with guys tonight—seriously, it was like Muscles R Us up in here, all filled-out chests and bulging arms with biceps upon biceps. Under other circumstances, Faith might take a moment to enjoy the view. But right now, she was looking for one particular meathead, and she happened to be related to him. Anger had been building the entire four-hour drive from Atlanta, and now it pulsed through her like the loud music, wanting to be set free.

Of all the stupidest, craziest, good-way-to-get-himself-killed moves. It was no wonder her brother hadn't told her what he was up to until she was on her way back to North Carolina, hours away from moving in with him and his family. Then Kaleb had thrown it out, all his words strung together. "By the way, I completed the SWAT program today and am a certified operator now. There's a party at the Rusty Anchor to celebrate, so you should swing by if you get into town in time."

And when Faith had opened her mouth to ask if he were serious, he'd said he had to go and hung up. But he'd later texted a picture of himself holding a certificate, his wife and daughter by his side, and told her the party was at seven. Like she'd actually want to celebrate something that would put him in even more danger than his current police job.

How can he do this to his family? His pregnant wife? His little girl? After all, Kaleb had seen firsthand what could happen in this line of work. He'd *promised* that he'd choose the safer path in his career. Faith hadn't wanted him to go into law enforcement in the first place, but *no*, he had to go and try to be a hero anyway. And now he was taking it to another level by joining a SWAT team? Why couldn't he let someone else's brother be a hero? Her family had given enough.

Faith scanned the room as she moved farther into it, taking a second to look from face to face. Finding her brother in a place she used to frequent ought to be easy, but the lights were dimmed, and there were so many guys, all dressed similarly in black T-shirts. Several had SWAT emblazoned on their chests in white, and others bore CORNELIUS SHERIFF'S DEPARTMENT in smaller letters over their shirt pocket.

Faith tipped onto her toes—this would be a lot easier if everyone here wasn't at least a foot taller than she was.

A guy approached her, beer bottle in one hand, smiling at her in that way guys do when they think they're good-looking enough to smile and get anything they want. "My friend and I were just talking about what a sausage fest this was, and then you came in." He ran his appraising gaze down her body, lingering on the V of her neckline.

Faith crossed her arms. "That works out, because I'm here for a weenie roast."

He put a protective hand over his package—probably without realizing he was doing it—but his smile widened. "Oh yeah. You're *definitely* coming to get a drink with me." He reached for her hand, but she jerked it away.

"I'm actually looking for Kaleb Fitzpatrick," she said as

cheers erupted over in the bar area, swallowing up her words.

Big and Beefy glanced toward the noise and then returned his attention to her and leaned down. "Fitzpatrick, you say?" This close, it was impossible not to notice just how good-looking he was. His almost black hair was disheveled in a careless way, he had thick, dark eyebrows, and his eyes were a strange shade of gray that had to be a trick of the light. One corner of his mouth turned up, as if he knew she liked what she saw. So maybe she did, but it wasn't like she'd go for a guy like him. The only thing worse than a guy with a hero complex was one who also had a huge ego.

"Do you know where he is or not?" she asked.

Despite the impatience she'd purposely put into her voice, the amusement in his features only grew. "Trust me, I'm more fun," he said, taking cocky to the next level with a simple eyebrow raise.

She blew out a breath. "Obviously you think pretty highly of yourself, but *trust me*, you don't wanna mess with me tonight."

He reached out and flicked the ends of her hair. "Actually, the very reason I came over here was to mess with you."

Faith made an extra-large eye roll. "Seriously, you're gonna have to do better than that."

Someone bumped into her from behind, causing her to stumble into the guy she'd been trying to break free from. He gripped her upper arms, his cold beer bottle pressing against her skin on one side as her hands braced against his chest, which she couldn't help but notice was rock solid.

The guy smelled like beer and broken promises, and still her heart fluttered the tiniest bit, the traitorous stirrings of attraction going through her gut. Breath caught in her throat, she froze in place instead of pushing away like she should.

Then she spotted her brother and her momentarily missing common sense started working again. She pulled back from Big and Beefy as Kaleb approached.

"Hey," Kaleb said, raising his voice over the din of multiple conversations and music. "Glad you could make it."

Faith clenched her fists, her earlier anger rising up again now that her brother was in front of her. "Well, you'll change your mind about that in about a second, because I came here to talk some sense into you, not congratulate you on being a well-trained idiot."

"Jeez, back down, girl," Big and Beefy said.

"Stay out of it," she shot back at him, then returned her gaze to Kaleb. "Why wasn't it enough to just be a cop? I don't understand why you'd need to go and join a SWAT team on top of it."

"Actually," Big and Beefy said, taking a sip from his beer, "that was my idea. Thought we could use more of an adventure."

She narrowed her eyes on him.

"Faith," Kaleb said, "Connor didn't mean—"

"*You're* the one who talked him into this?" She jabbed his chest with a finger. "Maybe *you* want to go throwing yourself in danger at every turn, but my brother has a little girl and a baby on the way. He has a wife to take care of. I know your type; you don't think of anyone else but yourself. And you"— she spun back to Kaleb—"you know the risks. How can you be such an idiot?" She hated the tears stinging her eyes. She blinked them back, refusing to lose it in the middle of the Rusty Anchor.

Big and Beefy—Connor, apparently—put his hand on her shoulder. "You need to relax. He's a hero."

"I wish he was a coward," she spat. All the heat seeped out of her, followed immediately by an overwhelming sense of failure. She wasn't sure what she thought would happen. Maybe that she'd yell and Kaleb would say he wasn't actually going to go through with it. Or that he'd at least acknowledge he was breaking promises. "Fine. Go celebrate. Just don't expect me to congratulate you." The hours in the car caught up to her all at once. Her eyes burned, her muscles were tight, and she needed something to eat, preferably with someone she didn't want to punch in the face. "I'm guessing Anna's around here somewhere."

Kaleb pointed over his shoulder. "Back corner in a booth." As Faith started away, he reached out and gave her arm a gentle squeeze. "It's going to be okay, Faithie. Going through the program means I'm better trained, and it's not like there's a lot of crime here. I just want to be prepared if there is. And the pay is better. I've got to think about that now that I'm going to have two kids to take care of."

A tight band formed around Faith's chest. "None of that will matter if you die before you get to see them grow up." She walked past him, trying to shove back her emotions so she could go find her pregnant sister-in-law and try to be strong for her. This was one of the reasons Faith had chosen to go to college a couple states over. She knew she was a bit irrational about her brother's career choice, but she couldn't help it.

And coming back had just brought up all the memories she wasn't ready to face.

· · ·

Connor watched the short, curvy blonde walk away from him and Kaleb. "That's your sister? She's dramatic. And kind of a—"

"Don't finish that." Kaleb smacked the back of Connor's head. "And stop checking out her ass."

Connor took one last glance. When he'd seen Faith walk into the bar, he couldn't look away. A moment before, he and Sullivan had been in a friendly argument over the tall brunette across the bar—Sullivan thought she was eyeing him, when she was clearly flirting with Connor—but then Faith had come in, and he was out of his seat before any of the other guys could hit on her. He hadn't expected her to be so damn prickly. As she'd been yelling, though, he'd had the strangest urge to kiss her so she'd shut up. Well, and so he could kiss her. But there were plenty of other girls out there—no way he'd want to deal with that emotional hurricane.

Although, it was kind of fun getting a rise out of her. In fact, it was the least bored he'd been with a woman in a while, which was sad but true. And for all her talk, she was about to be putty in his hands before her brother showed up.

Kaleb cleared his throat.

Connor slowly pulled his gaze off Faith and shook his fuzzy head. "Give me a break—I'm drunk."

"Just go point your wasted self at someone else. She's already pissed off and going to be impossible to deal with. I don't need you adding to the mess."

Connor raised his hands, palms up. "I got it. Leave your sister alone. Now, let's go get another drink." Whether Faith liked it or not, they were celebrating. And they *were* heroes. The training had been killer—obstacle courses, shooting drills, sleep deprivation—and they'd survived. Together. Kaleb was one of his best friends, and his wife, Anna, was cool, too, which was why he liked hanging at their place so much—their house felt like his second home. As chill as Anna usually was, though, Connor could tell she hadn't been thrilled about the SWAT thing, either.

Just another reason why he was in no hurry to settle down.

• • •

Faith slid into the back booth where Anna was seated. The table hid the bottom half of her belly, but the top was clearly rounded, and her sister-in-law had that pregnant-lady glow people talked about.

Faith glanced out at the rowdy sea of guys filling the bar and then back at Anna. "I don't want to stress you out, but how are you not freaking out about Kaleb doing this?"

Anna shrugged. "I wasn't exactly happy about it at first, but we discussed all the pros and cons and why he wanted to do it. Plus, I've had longer than a day to process it. I told him to tell you earlier, and even thought about doing so myself, but I didn't want to get in the middle of it."

Faith gritted her teeth. Of course Kaleb had waited to tell her, because he'd known how upset she'd be. She and Kaleb were both stubborn, and they'd fought plenty growing up. But they were also close, and if anyone messed with her, he made sure it never happened again. He'd always taken care of her and even let her boss him around a bit. Too bad he'd grown out of that, because she'd really like to force him to change careers.

Faith picked up the flip chart on the table with all the drinks and started turning the pages without really looking at the brews it bragged about. "If anything bad goes down, he's now the first line of defense. That's got to worry you at least a little."

"Of course it does. But I've never seen him so happy. He's proud that he made it through. I'm proud of him, too."

Faith reached the end of the drink menu and then shoved it aside. "If it were the guy I loved…I couldn't do it."

"Oh, never say never," Anna said.

"I'm saying it. *Never.* I'm going to find a nice nerdy guy to settle down with. Whether it's math or science or just an obsessive amount of *Star Wars* gear and love for role-playing games, I don't care. I'm not even giving a second glance at law enforcement or military guys."

Anna cracked a smile. "Then you better not look around.

Being surrounded by all these ripped guys only makes me feel even more whalelike." She put a hand on the top of her belly.

"You look great, and I can't wait to meet the little guy." Faith scooted forward and put her hand on her sister-in-law's tummy, hoping to feel her nephew moving around. "I am happy about that part of living closer. And I can't wait to see Ella."

"She's been talking for weeks about you coming to live with us."

Faith pictured her little niece—chubby cheeks, strawberry-blond curls, and the same green eyes Faith and Kaleb had gotten from their dad. She'd wrapped Faith around her finger from day one.

"And how are you doing with…everything?" Anna asked.

Everything. AKA, the fact that she'd dumped her savings into a down payment on a condo so she and Jeff could move in together, only to discover him cheating on her in their brand-new bed, forcing her to rearrange all of her plans. "I'm just glad everything's finally taken care of. The title's signed over, and after the attorney fees, I should slowly get my money back, one payment from the jackass at a time." Faith folded her arms on the table. "I appreciate you letting me stay with you while I look for a new place. It should be two months, three tops."

"You're welcome to stay as long as you need. It'll be nice to have someone around to talk to. Kaleb's gone a lot, and as much as I love Ella, she's not the best conversationalist. Unless you want to discuss princesses or cartoons." Anna shook her head. "I don't know how she got to be so girlie."

Anna was a T-shirt-and-jeans type girl. Somehow Ella came out with a love for all things frilly and pink. A waitress came by and Faith ordered a burger and fries, the same thing she'd always ordered here. The same thing Dad had always ordered here. It was too packed to get a good look around, but she saw enough to know that the place was still the same. They probably even had Dad's picture and the framed article about him hanging on the wall behind the bar. It'd hurt Faith to see it, but it'd hurt even more if it weren't there.

She'd be tempted to go check it out, but Kaleb and that Connor guy were at the bar, and she wasn't sure she was ready to dive into the past anyway. So she talked to Anna while she waited for her food and all through her meal. She could almost block out the reason she was in the Rusty Anchor and just focus on how nice it was to be back in Cornelius. But of course then she'd see a guy with a stupid SWAT shirt and get mad and scared all over again.

Maybe coming back was a mistake. But after everything had fallen apart in Atlanta—leaving her feeling like a crushed fool, as well as low on funds—she'd needed an escape. Dr. Schaeffer's call asking if she wanted a spot in the predoctoral clinical psychology internship he was heading up was too good an offer to refuse.

After the waitress took away her empty plate, Kaleb showed up. He scooted into the booth next to his wife and leaned back, his eyes on Faith. "You still pissed?"

Faith sighed. "Not pissed so much anymore. Just…I don't like it. I'm never going to be happy about you being a cop, and this is a whole new level of scary for me."

"I understand, I do. When Dad died…" Kaleb glanced at the bar area and she could see the way his throat was working. It made a lump rise in her own. "I want him to be proud of me. And I want to keep people safe. My wife…" He put his hand on Anna's stomach. "My kids. You." He exhaled. "Just try to understand."

The big, puppy-dog eyes he flashed at her made it impossible to stay mad. At *him*, anyway. She caught sight of Connor seated at the bar and decided to aim all her anger his way. At least then she'd have someone to blame.

"I'll try. That's the best I can do right now." Faith rolled her neck from side to side, still stiff and tired from her day. "How long do we have to stay and watch all the cavemen congratulate themselves?"

Kaleb laughed. "We can go home right now." He looked at Anna, who nodded, and then they got up and started out of the bar.

Faith swore she could feel someone looking at her, so she glanced over her shoulder.

Connor was staring right at her. He raised his beer and winked.

What a conceited—

Faith ran right into the open door.

It was the kind of move that's impossible to hide, where you grasp for something to keep you up and only get air. She finally got control of her body and focused on stepping *around* the door this time. Right before it closed, she caught sight of Connor, still staring.

And judging from the smug grin on his face, he'd definitely enjoyed the show.

• • •

Connor smiled into his beer. That girl put on a good act, but she was attracted to him—so much so, she ran right into the door. A quick swirl of his bottle and then he tipped it up and downed the rest of its contents. Sure, he'd originally thought he should avoid her, but her fiery personality had him wanting another chance to mess with her. Faith was a challenge wrapped in a hot body, and that happened to be his favorite type of challenge.

"Hey." It was the twiggy brunette he'd been arguing over with Sullivan earlier. She breathed more than said the word as she settled onto the stool next to him.

Connor flashed his signature make-the-ladies-crazy half smile. "Hey."

She giggled. Then stared at him, blinking her brown, bloodshot eyes. Apparently he was supposed to come up with the conversation. He glanced toward the door, which was stupid, because Kaleb's little sister had left.

Ugh. She was his best friend's sister. Probably a bad idea—no, *definitely* a bad idea.

Of course, he specialized in bad ideas. He thought about when she'd stumbled into him and the little gasp noise she'd made. How her curves felt against his body, and the heat that had wound through his veins and was rising up again at the memory.

"…Sarah. And you are?" The brunette was leaning close. Her hand was on his knee. Did she say her name was Sarah? She was pretty. Maybe a little boring, which hadn't ever concerned him all that much before, but lately, didn't even seem worth the minimal effort. It'd been a while, though. Long by his usual standards.

"Connor," he said when he realized she was still waiting for his name. More giggling. Her hand slid a little higher.

Time to make a decision. Which bad idea was he going to go for tonight?

Chapter Two

Connor felt the bed shift. He could feel the steady stare, but he didn't open his eyes—he barely breathed, not wanting to give away the fact that he was awake. He wondered how long it'd take until she gave up on him and left the bed. He was too hungover to deal with it.

A wet tongue dragged across his face.

The bark that followed was so loud it made his ears ring. Then came more licking.

He shoved his dog's face away, groaning as the bright light pierced his eyeballs. "Fine, I'm up. I'm up."

Connor's two-year-old German shepherd sat there breathing on him, because she'd figured out if she took off too soon he'd just go back to sleep and she'd have to wake him up all over again. This was one of the reasons he'd turned down the offer from the brunette girl at the bar last night. He already had a needy girl at home.

Okay, that wasn't the only reason. He'd thought that after going through training, after accomplishing another step in his desired career path, he'd get back to feeling like himself.

But he still felt like something deeper was missing from his life. Hell, he'd even considered letting his friends Wes and Dani set him up a few months back, to see if he could try a serious relationship. But that'd fallen through, and he'd told himself he was relieved.

Penny barked again—so damn loud—and nudged him with her wet nose.

"I drank too much last night, Pen. Does that mean nothing to you?"

Penny whimpered and he swore she looked at the clock, as if to say, *Can't you see we're already thirty minutes behind schedule? Get your lazy ass out of bed and take me running already.*

Connor slowly sat up, promised himself he'd never drink that much again, and pulled on warm-ups, a T-shirt, and his sneakers.

The cool morning air helped wake him up the rest of the way, though he was still foggier than usual. Penny didn't take it easy on him, tugging him hard toward Lake Norman. Running was a release, a way to get everything off his mind and start the day fresh. But today it just wasn't doing it for him. When he tried to turn around a mile shorter than usual— today was more of a three- than a five-mile day—Penny didn't budge, pulling against her leash and whimpering. Finally, with the promise of an extra doggy treat when they got home, he convinced her to turn around. He had about a mile to go when he caught sight of the blonde jogging ahead of him.

He swore he'd stared at that same ass at the Rusty Anchor. Despite the fogginess, that was one thing he distinctly remembered from last night. He took a couple long strides to close the distance and get a closer look. Yep, it was definitely Kaleb's little sister. Hair pulled up in a messy bun, cheeks flushed, black yoga pants showing off her shapely butt. Man, he loved yoga pants. He quickened his pace to catch up with her.

Faith glanced at Penny as she started to pass her up.

"Nice morning for a jog, isn't it?" Connor asked, forcing as much cheeriness into his voice as he could manage.

"Yeah, it i—" Faith nearly tripped over her feet when her gaze landed on him.

He grabbed her arm to help steady her. "Careful, or you'll have skinned knees to go with that mark on your face. You know, from where you ran into the door last night while checking me out."

She jerked her arm away from him. "I was not... It was dark and... You're so cocky, you know that?"

"It's part of my charm."

"You don't have any charm." Faith crouched down to pet Penny as she glared at him, and his dog snuggled right up to her. "A cop with a German shepherd. How cliché of you." The verbal jab was canceled out by the adoration in her voice. More for the dog than him, probably, but he liked to think it was a little him, too.

Faith scratched behind Penny's ears. "Poor doggy. I bet it's hard living with an ego that big, isn't it? You ever need a break, you come find me."

"You're staying with Kaleb and Anna, right?" Connor asked.

Faith glanced up, one of her eyebrows quirking higher than the other.

"If Penny needs a place to escape, she needs to know where you'll be." He reached down and patted his dog, and her dark eyes and muzzle moved back and forth between him and Faith.

The breeze caught hold of the pale strands coming loose from Faith's bun. One of the strands stuck to her lip and she quickly swiped it away. But now he was looking at her full bottom lip and how it had a slight indentation in the middle.

And since he was crouched down petting Penny, he was close enough to really take in Faith's features, things he hadn't noticed in the dim bar last night. She had high cheekbones, startling green eyes, and a cute little beauty mark above one eyebrow.

He thought about how bored he'd been with women lately. He had a feeling he'd be anything but with this girl. She was feisty, and by all appearances, couldn't stand him. He wasn't sure what it said that he found himself intrigued by that, but he was.

"I'd better get on with my jog," Faith suddenly said, straightening. And then she was off and running. He wanted to catch up and tease her a little more. See if her cheeks flushed the way he vaguely recalled them doing last night. But then again, the view was nice from back here, and he knew something she probably didn't…

He was going over to Kaleb's later today. And there, it wouldn't be so easy for her to run away from him.

• • •

Faith wandered the familiar streets of Cornelius, noting everything that had changed in the past six years. Most places were the same, with the exception of an upgrade here and there. Lake Norman glittered in the distance, coming into view between the buildings. She'd spent her childhood on that lake. Boating. Swimming. Fishing.

Flyers advertising the upcoming Fall Festival hung on the lampposts. They'd close off this section of town and set up booths in the middle of the street, leading all the way to Magnolia Park, where there'd be live music and contests. Faith had already signed up for the Fallen Officer 5K that'd take place early that morning. It was why she'd dragged herself out of bed and forced herself to go run—she wished she were in better shape, but she wanted to contribute however she could, so she'd walk the end of the race if she had to. Afterward, she'd go to the festival and fill up on delicious, artery-clogging food. Anna was going to set up a booth for the pottery she made, too. She'd been talking for months about how excited she was to have her vases, bowls, and plates on display for such a big event and how she hoped to make some extra money before the baby arrived.

Bigfish Bait and Tackle shop came into view, and Faith quickened her pace. The shop belonged to family friends, and while she was closer to Paul's age, she and Brynn had suffered through fishing excursions together. The guys used to roll their eyes and complain about the smell when she and Brynn would sit on deck and paint their nails—the guys were covered in fish guts half the time, but apparently nail polish was too stinky to handle. They'd kept in touch through Facebook, but Faith hadn't seen Paul or Brynn since she'd left six years ago.

I hope they're in the shop today. If not, she'd ask Paul Senior how to find them. Her stay here would be much easier with familiar friends to hang out with. As she neared the shop, she spotted a girl with dark hair delivering a grape soda to a guy sitting at a table, laptop out in front of him.

Faith's heart dropped. If someone had converted Bigfish into a trendy café, she might cry. Not that she was in a huge need of fishing supplies, but Dad used to love the place. He'd go in to "grab just one thing" and end up talking to Paul Senior for hours. Losing little places he loved felt like losing even more of him.

"Faith Fitzpatrick?" The girl straightened, and Faith realized it was Brynn. Her hair was dyed dark, but her features were still the same. Though the cut and color highlighted them and fit her more vintage style.

"I hardly recognized you," Faith said, meeting Brynn

halfway for a hug. "You look great."

"Thanks. You, too."

"For a second, I was afraid someone had turned Bigfish into a café."

Brynn grinned at the guy seated at the table. "*Someone* thinks it's a café that serves grape soda." She bounced on the balls of her feet, joy clear on her features. "This is Sawyer. My boyfriend."

"Weren't you on the football team at Hough High?"

Sawyer pushed out from the green wrought iron table and stood, wrapping an arm around Brynn's waist like it was second nature. "That was me. Back before I learned to appreciate the arts. And awesome girls who were passionate about them."

Brynn's grin widened, and he kissed her cheek.

Faith couldn't help but stare for a moment. She could clearly see how in love Brynn and Sawyer were. That was what she wanted: a guy who was serious about settling down. A guy who wouldn't look around at other girls and see what he was missing. She'd been so stupid in her relationship with Jeff, thinking she'd tamed a player. From now on, she was staying far, far away from those types.

"I'll go get Paul," Brynn said. "He's engaged now, and I'm sure he'll tell you all about his bride to be. If you need an out, just give me the signal."

Faith laughed. "I forgot about the signal." Back in the day, when her family used to hang out with the McAdamses, she, Brynn, and Paul would rub the side of their nose with one finger and then come up with a reason to escape. They'd sneak out to the lake or just relax in the backyard. The scent of charred meat would still be hanging in the air from Dad barbecuing and Mom's laughter would occasionally ring out—she used to have the loudest laugh.

But those were the happy years. The before.

The lake water-scented air that'd smelled so fresh moments before turned sour. She'd thought the years away would've made everything easier—that she'd dealt with the past through college-level psychology classes and real-world experience. But it was different when the past was in every place she looked. It was why she'd run from here as soon as she'd gotten out of high school. When things went bad in Atlanta, she'd fled there, too. So much for facing things like a grown-up.

Paul McAdams stepped out of the store and grinned. His brown hair was shorter than he used to wear it in high school, and he'd filled out quite a bit. "Why, Shorty Fitzpatrick. Long time no see."

He pulled Faith into a hug, and the anxiety that'd been working its way through her eased. Whenever she thought about home, she tended to focus on the bad memories and sorrow. She'd forgotten how friendly people were here. How nice it was to be around others who knew the real her. Everyone who'd known Daddy had come together to try to help her family. They'd done everything they could. Faith appreciated it, and she knew Mom had, too. But it hadn't changed the fact that they were missing someone who should've been with them still.

"We've got to plan a fishing trip," Paul said, and Faith returned to the present. She forced a smile and nodded. But she couldn't stop thinking about how this sleepy, innocent-looking town had taken her dad.

And she couldn't help thinking it might take Kaleb next.

• • •

Faith could hear deep voices in the living room, Kaleb's and another. She couldn't make out the words, but Anna was talking with them. Faith closed her laptop and set it on the nightstand. After several hours searching through pictures of apartments, her eyes burned and the spot between her shoulder blades ached.

She stepped over the boxes she wasn't sure whether to put away or leave packed. Anna and Kaleb both said she could stay as long as she wanted, which was nice, but she wouldn't feel like she was starting over until she had her own place. Preferably close to the UNC School of Medicine, where she'd be doing her internship. Maybe living in Charlotte would be enough to get away from all the memories but close enough to stay connected to her brother and his family.

Again she was glad Dr. Schaeffer had reached out to her. He was a long-time friend of the family; had set up her, Mom, and Kaleb with a nice counselor to help deal with Dad's passing; and had advised her when she told him she was interested in becoming a counselor. Clinical spots were difficult to find, and she couldn't wait to get started. Having a couple of months off had sounded nice at first, especially after six straight years of studying day and night. But with all the memories rising up, she might need a temporary job to keep herself busy.

Faith stepped into the hallway and walked toward the scent of food, garlic, and spices—whatever it was, it smelled amazing and made her stomach growl.

She froze in her tracks when she spotted Connor. He caught her eye and grinned. She hated how her heart fluttered. Hated that all day she'd been thinking about seeing him out running with his dog.

It should be illegal for guys to be that good-looking. She'd always gone for the wrong kind of guys, and her heart had the scars to prove it. But this last time, she really had learned her lesson. From now on, she was choosing sweet, humble guys. No exceptions. And *definitely* no guys who looked or acted like Connor.

"I was just about to call for you," Anna said, glancing her way. "Dinner's all but ready. Kaleb, can you grab the plates for me?" They disappeared into the kitchen. Ella was crashed on the couch after a long day of playing hard and loud, her blond curls covering most of her face. She was somehow able to sleep through the talking and the sound of plates and cupboard doors banging.

Connor stepped toward Faith, and she had the irrational urge to bolt in the other direction. Or maybe it was rational. He could pick her up and break her in half, after all. "You ran off this morning before I could—"

"Talk about the giant mark on my face?" she asked, crossing her arms.

He grinned. "No, I believe I covered that. But we could talk about it more if you want."

She tilted her head. "Ha-ha." Her muscles tensed, her guard rising from him being so close. She needed to control this situation. Show she absolutely *wasn't* interested.

"Don't feel bad. Happens all the time when girls look at me, actually." He took another step toward her and lowered his voice. "What I'm trying to say is I was really drunk last night, and sometimes when I'm drunk I act a little stupid."

"So what's your excuse right now?" She figured the bitchier she was, the sooner he'd see she was more trouble than he wanted. Might as well nip it in the bud now, especially with how inescapable he was apparently going to be.

His gray, nearly translucent eyes lit up as a smile stretched across his lips. "I guess I'm just so stunned by your beauty."

She shook her head. "Back when I was young and naive, I might've fallen for a guy like you. But I'm smarter now, so go try your lines on someone else."

"But you're the only one here."

She started around him but he held out his arm, blocking her path. "And even if this room were filled with women, I'd still flirt with you. Just so you know."

She worked to keep her voice even—bored, almost. "Well, just so *you* know, I don't fall for lines, and it takes more than good looks to impress me."

"So you think I'm good-looking." He reached out and flicked the ends of her hair, the same way he had last night. "It's big of you to finally admit it."

Irritation wound through her, tightening the spot between her shoulders. "I think you're the most frustrating person I've ever met. I'm still mad you talked my brother into something stupid and then you think you can just come in here and hit on me?"

"I *was* trying to apologize for last night. But now that you mention the hitting on you thing…" He gave a casual shrug. "I could probably get down with that."

"You're an ass."

"And you have a nice ass."

Faith stared back at him, her jaw clenched. She was wrong. She'd never dealt with this kind of guy before. He was a whole new level of cocky jerk.

"Are you guys coming?" Anna asked, sticking her head out the archway of the kitchen.

Connor gestured Faith ahead of him. He put his hand on her back as they started to walk toward the dining room, and she slapped it away.

She heard his low chuckle behind her, and she wondered if Kaleb would be mad or proud if she turned around and decked the guy. Why was her brother even friends with him?

As soon as she sat down, Connor scooted his chair right next to hers. She shook her head, doing her best to ignore his hulking presence as they passed around the food.

"This tortellini is amazing, Anna," Connor said after they'd all dug in. "And the marinara sauce tastes as authentic as the kind my mama makes."

Anna waved off his comment, but her entire face lit up.

How was everyone blind to how full of crap Connor was? He was one of those guys who said whatever it took to get his way, then burned you without a second thought—she'd know. She'd been fooled by several before, though Jeff definitely took the cake. Or condo and the future she'd planned, as it were.

Faith swallowed her bite of cheese-filled pasta—okay, it was pretty amazing—and turned to Kaleb. "By the way, I saw Paul and Brynn today. You never told me they were running the bait shop now."

Kaleb bit into a breadstick. "They run the bait shop now."

Faith nudged his leg with the toe of her shoe. "So helpful."

He smiled, his cheek puffed up on one side because of the bread. "Not like I'm ever free to go fishing anymore. Maybe with training over, I'll have some extra time."

Anna raised her eyebrows. "Oh really?"

"I mean, after I take my beautiful wife out. Who wants to go fishing when that's an option?"

Anna gave him a gentle shove, and he winked at her.

"I'm sure your job will only get busier now," Faith said. "How's the whole"—she took a deep breath and forced it out—"SWAT thing work, anyway?"

Connor's cup clinked against the table as he set it down. "It means we do our usual job at the police station most days, but if there's ever an emergency, we're on call."

Faith kept her attention on Kaleb. "Will they call you for an emergency in Charlotte?"

"Depends on how big the emergency," Connor answered. "A few years ago, three other departments in Mecklenberg County formed a multijurisdictional SWAT team—Pineville, Matthews, and Mint Hill. I've been on Captain to do the same thing for North Meck."

Finally, Faith couldn't not look at him anymore.

He rested his knee against hers, and she doubted it was unintentional. "It's about making the most of our resources," Connor continued. "We didn't have enough guys to make a full SWAT team, but all together, we're able to increase response time and have a bigger pool to choose from. If something happened in Huntersville, Mooresville, or here in Cornelius, we'd be called to the site, instead of having to wait for guys from Charlotte. Now, the Lake Norman area is protected." He flashed her a toothpaste commercial grin. "Don't you feel safer?"

Faith refused to admit that it did make her feel safer, knowing trained men were nearby. Because it didn't change the fact that her brother was the *opposite* of safer.

"There's really not much chance of us going to the bigger cities, but if we're needed, we'll go." Kaleb glanced at Anna before looking back at Faith. "We trained for extreme circumstances. But we'll mostly be doing the same thing. Just think, if Dad were trained like I am n—"

"Please," Faith said, holding up her hand. "Don't go there." She'd spent years going over the what-ifs, and it only made her feel worse. "You'll never convince me that this is the safest option for you, because it's simply not true."

"But if—" Connor started.

She pointed her fork at him. "You don't get a say in this at all. You have no idea what it's like, and this is a family matter."

"Faith," Kaleb said in the scolding tone he'd used when he was in charge of her in high school. But she was old enough to make her own decisions now.

"It's okay," Connor said. "She's right. I didn't have to deal with what you two did, and I get why it worries her." He turned his eyes on her. "You should probably know, though, that I consider Kaleb and his family my family, too."

Compared to all the bull crap he spouted, that actually

sounded genuine, and his expression matched. Appearing happy he'd cleared that up, he shoveled another forkful of pasta in his mouth.

Faith couldn't help leaning in and saying, "Guess that makes us like brother and sister, then." A smug sense of satisfaction ran through her when Connor nearly choked on his bite of food.

Point one to me.

"Uncle Connor?" Ella stood in the doorway of the kitchen, her blond curls mashed on the side where her face was also pink from being against the couch.

"Ella Ballerina!" He spun around in his chair, and she ran forward and launched herself into his arms. "How are you today?"

"Dood," Ella said, putting her chubby hands on the sides of his face.

It was quickly becoming clear that Connor spent a lot of time here. Not that Ella was that hard to win over. Gum or anything involving sugar or princesses usually did the trick. But her face lit up as Connor bounced her on his knee, and he was clearly comfortable with her as well.

He smoothed a hand down Ella's hair and a crack formed in the wall Faith had built around her heart. And that simply wouldn't do. He actually went out of his way to form a SWAT team. He was full of himself...

Okay, so he was sorta beautiful, with his olive skin and stupid muscles and sexy, dark hair. And he was super sweet to her niece.

Point two to him.

"You hungry?" Connor asked, and Ella bobbed her head.

Anna started to get up and Kaleb put his hand on her shoulder. "I got it." He took Ella from Connor, put her in her booster chair, and gave her a plate of food.

"So, Faith?" Connor said, glancing at her. "Why'd you

move back here?"

"I just got my master's in psychology, and I'm starting an internship at the UNC School of Medicine in the fall, where I'll complete my clinical hours."

"Psychology. Interesting."

She didn't know what he meant by that, and she wasn't sure she wanted to. As she'd gone through the curriculum, she'd sometimes felt like a fraud, studying all the information on talking about your problems and confronting your past, when she still hid from hers. But she liked to think that she'd used what she'd learned and gotten better at dealing over the years.

Didn't mean she was perfect.

Connor draped his arm over the back of her chair. "Maybe you can analyze me sometime."

Kaleb cleared his throat and shot a pointed look at Connor. Connor shrugged and held his hands up for a moment before dropping them to his sides.

Interesting. That point might go to Kaleb, but I think it'll work in my favor.

They made small talk through the rest of the meal. Ella was covered in marinara sauce by the end. Kaleb went to bathe her, and Faith insisted on doing the dishes so Anna could kick up her swollen ankles.

Surprisingly, Connor offered to help. Faith rinsed plates and set them in the dishwasher, focusing on the task, so she wouldn't focus on the way the muscles in his arms flexed as he cleared the table. He set the dishes in the rack of the washer and turned, running his eyes down her. "You know, you've got the kind of legs that make me wanna be pants."

Faith burst out laughing. "That does not seriously work on girls."

"It does."

"Maybe desperate drunk girls."

Connor leaned in so close she could feel his warmth. "It's working on you right now."

"Sorry. You'll have to do better than that." She pushed him back with a hand to his chest and placed the last of the cups in the top rack.

"Okay, the line, while true, was more of a joke. But we should grab a drink sometime."

Faith drew her eyebrows together. "That's better? Here I thought you were some kind of player and you don't have any game."

He put his hands on the counter, on either side of her. "Damn, you're as cold as you are hot."

"I don't even know what that means. Maybe I should just call my brother in here and see what he thinks."

Connor's smug grin faded. So there *had* been some kind of discussion. Within seconds he recovered though. "You need permission from your big brother?"

"No. I need a desire to go. And unfortunately for you, I'm immune to guys like you." She patted his arm and moved past him. She could feel his eyes on her as she started the dishwasher, but she didn't look at him again. As annoying as it was, confident men were sexy. Of course, they also used their confidence on any and all women, which was how they'd gotten so sure of themselves in the first place.

Ella came bounding into the room, dressed in a pink nightgown with Disney princesses on the front. This time, Faith was the one she ran to. Faith pulled her niece into her arms. "Should we braid your hair?"

"And paint nails?"

"Sure." Faith grinned at Connor. "You want to paint nails, too? We've got a glittery pink that's to die for."

"Oh, I'm man enough to pull it off, but I'd better get going. Gotta get up early for my morning run. You wanna meet up? You did promise to give Penny a break from me."

Faith shook her head. "Nice try. But I like to run alone." *Where I can hold my side and gasp for air halfway through.*

"Suit yourself." Connor leaned down and kissed Ella's forehead. "See you later, Ella Ballerina," he said. Then he pressed his lips to Faith's cheek, and his low voice rumbled in her ear. "Till next time."

Faith hugged her niece tight, telling herself that the goose bumps spreading across her skin didn't mean a thing.

Nope, not a thing.

Chapter Three

Faith woke up to the sound of knocking. She glanced around, trying to get her bearings. Last night she'd decided to watch a movie. Since she hadn't wanted to keep anyone awake—or risk waking up Ella—she'd used Kaleb's wireless headphones. They were on the floor now and Faith's neck was kinked from sleeping on the couch.

When the knocking came again, Faith padded to the door and swung it open. Connor stood on the other side. He wore a light blue collared shirt with a police logo, black pants, and a belt with all the bells and whistles, including a gun and handcuffs.

In other words, he looked like uniformed police hotness, and she wasn't entirely uninterested in being cuffed. *Wait. That's a bad thought. I don't mean it.* She took him in again, her throat suddenly dry. Well, she didn't exactly *not* mean it, but she knew better than to *want* it. Or something like that. She was still too asleep to think clearly.

Oh no. I can only imagine what I look like. Not that it mattered, since his type was obviously women in general, but she'd rather not be aware of the fact that her hair was sticking up on one side. Or that she was wearing her worn-out I love carbs T-shirt. Especially since it had holes in it. It probably looked like all the carbs in the house were gone and she'd taken bites out of it in desperation.

At least her shorts showed off her legs. Maybe he could focus on that. *Wait—when's the last time I shaved?*

"Morning," Connor said, and she had the unnerving feeling that he could read her every thought.

She crossed her arms and squinted at the bright outside light. "What are you doing here?"

"Picking up your brother. We carpool." He shot her a way-too-perky smile. "In case you haven't heard, it's good for the environment."

"I've… It's… You… Ugh…" She ran a hand over her face, most likely smearing yesterday's makeup even more.

Connor stepped past her, his chest brushing against her arm. "Wow, I'm disappointed, Blondie. You usually have much better comebacks."

She frowned at him. "I just woke up. Haven't even had coffee yet."

"I've already run five miles, plus showered—where I was naked, because I know you were wondering."

She rolled her eyes. "How 'bout you run one more mile and get the hell away from me?"

"And leave the warmth of your sunny disposition? No thanks."

Faith's brain was too fuzzy to come up with a response. So she simply turned and walked away. She knocked as quietly as possible on Kaleb and Anna's bedroom door. Kaleb popped his head out, his hair still damp from the shower.

"Your ass of a friend is here," she said.

"Can you tell him I'll be right out? My alarm didn't go off, but all I have to do is throw on my uniform and I'll be good to go."

Faith groaned. She really didn't want to go back. If she pulled up her hair or washed her face, Connor would notice and think she cared what he thought. So she zombie shuffled back down the hall. "He's running late. It'll be a few minutes." She flopped on the couch and pulled the blanket over herself, hoping he'd at least take the hint to leave her alone while he waited.

The couch sank with Connor's weight a moment later. "You're not going to offer me breakfast?"

She kicked at him, and he grabbed her foot. She was about to jerk it away, but then he started massaging it, and *oh. My. Gosh!* A sigh was trying to escape her lips and she had to clamp them to hold it in.

"So, what's the plan for today?" he asked.

Faith lowered the blanket to look at him. Was he really going to act like this was normal? She really should pull away. When he let go, she told herself it wasn't disappointment running through her. But then he grabbed her other foot and put it in his lap, working his magic.

"I, uh, think I'm running errands with Anna and Ella." Wow, her life sounded so exciting. Maybe that was for the best. He'd realize she was boring and stop hitting on her.

Footsteps sounded in the hallway, and Connor leaned over her, his hard body pressed against her legs. He grabbed her cell phone off the side table and typed something into it. "There. Now you can give me a call." He placed the phone in her hand. "I get off work at six."

He stood as Kaleb came into the room.

Then they left, leaving Faith wondering what the hell just happened.

And why she hadn't done a better job of shutting it down.

• • •

Connor glanced toward the house one last time before climbing in the squad car, Faith's image burned into his mind. When she'd first opened the door... Well, it'd looked like she'd just had a romp in bed, and he wanted to be the one rolling around in the sheets with her.

His breath went shallow thinking about it.

Kaleb laughed, and Connor tucked the image of Faith away for later—when he wasn't with her brother. "What's so funny?"

"I was a little worried about Faith being interested in you, and that I'd have to explain you didn't do relationships or worry you'd try to sleep with her. But she's totally immune. In fact, I'm pretty sure she hates you."

"She doesn't hate me. We worked things out last night when we cleaned up the kitchen together."

"Funny, because she told me, 'Your ass of a friend is here.'" Kaleb laughed again, and Connor gripped the steering wheel. It wasn't *that* funny. And his insistence that Faith wouldn't go for him only made him want to prove Kaleb wrong. Not to mention that the more interactions he had with her, the more he wanted. There was something about the way her eyes lit up when she talked to him, a sarcastic comment always at the ready.

Maybe it was time to try something new.

"I've had relationships," Connor said.

"Dude, I think you had one that lasted a month since I've known you. It's not like I care; as long as the girl you're after isn't my sister, do whatever with whoever you want. But it's my job to keep Faith from getting hurt again. The girl attracts total tools, and I can't tell you how many times I've had to restrain myself from kicking the shit out of a few of them."

Total tools. Connor frowned, wondering if he were included in that. Granted, he probably wouldn't want a guy like himself to date his sister, but he was always upfront about what it was, no pretending it'd ever be more. It was mutually beneficial for all parties involved, and he'd had no complaints from women so far, even though he could tell some had wanted more. Whenever things reached that point, he'd end it as nicely as possible. No hurt feelings on either side. No messy complications that'd end in screaming matches.

"The last guy, though..." Kaleb continued, his hand curling into a fist. "If Anna hadn't talked me down, I would've driven to Atlanta and probably got myself arrested."

Usually his partner was coolheaded, but Connor had seen him get angry enough to know he could beat a guy to a bloody pulp—not to mention his sharp-shooting skills. The last thing he wanted to do was piss off the guy who was supposed to have his back every day.

Then there was the fact that their father was one of his heroes. He'd been surprised when he first found out Kaleb was Officer Fitzpatrick's son, but the guy had quickly become his best friend. So despite the fact that he'd had trouble getting Faith off his mind from the first moment he saw her, he needed to keep himself in check. Mess with her, sure—because that was way too fun to give up—but he'd keep things light. Friendly.

Shouldn't be too hard, considering she apparently hated him anyway.

. . .

Faith loved her niece more than anything. But when the girl wasn't crying, she was screaming or giggling or running around in circles. Anna's errands had taken forever, from the post office to the bank to a stop at the grocery store, and so Ella missed her regular nap. She refused to sleep, was cranky because of it, and by five thirty, Faith needed a break. So she headed to the Rusty Anchor. The other night she'd been angry at her brother and distracted by the crowd, so she hadn't taken the time to really be there.

As soon as she walked into the bar, she let herself take in the familiar dark wood paneling, the country song overhead, how she could think of a memory at nearly every table. It was Daddy's go-to place at the end of the day, where he knew everyone and they all knew him. She remembered thinking he must be practically famous, especially when they gave him 20 percent off every bill—the "serviceman special." Whenever Mom found out he'd taken Faith there, she'd tell him it was an inappropriate place to bring a teenage girl.

Dad would say, "It's not like I ordered her a beer. I do know a little something about the law, you know."

Then Mom would huff and Dad would go over and wrap his arms around her, and she'd give up being mad. But she'd strongly suggest they choose a different place next time.

And the next time, they'd go right back to the Rusty Anchor. The fries were the best—there was no arguing that.

Faith approached the bar and let her eyes drift to the spot she'd been both anticipating and fearing looking at. Daddy's picture was still there, right next to the framed article about him, the hero policeman.

The picture was of him in his navy uniform, his dirty-blond hair combed back, big smile on his face. A twinge went through Faith's chest as she thought about the fact that he never got a chance to grow old. See her graduate high school or college. Get to know his daughter-in-law or granddaughter. The hollow ache she always got when she thought of him opened up, sucking happiness out of the space around her. She'd always been a daddy's girl. At one point, she'd even told him she wanted to grow up to be a cop like him. She hoped he wasn't disappointed she'd gone another way. Or that she'd gotten mad at Kaleb for following through on his promise to do the same thing.

"Can I help you?" the girl behind the bar asked.

Faith pulled her gaze off Daddy's picture and ordered the burger and fries. She got the house beer, because that's what Dad would've ordered. As the bartender was filling up her glass, Boyd Elkins came over. He owned the bar and had gone to school with Dad.

"Ain't you Paddy Fitzpatrick's little girl?"

Faith nodded. "Hi, Boyd."

"I can hardly believe it. You used to be just a little thing. Guess you never grew much," he said, eyeing her height. Well, nice to see the guy still liked to hassle everyone. Some things never changed, and there was as much comfort as grief in that. "How's your mom?"

Surely Kaleb must've updated him now and then, but she supposed it was an easier question to ask her. "Good. My grandparents are happy to have her, and she likes Virginia."

His eyebrows drew together as if he just couldn't compute liking somewhere else. Most people who grew up here didn't know why anyone left. She supposed most of them didn't have a reason to. Boyd patted the waitress on the shoulder. "Her drink's on me. And give her the serviceman discount on anything else she orders."

"You don't have to..." Faith started, but he was already moving away, off to help another customer. She took her drink to the corner to wait for her food. She liked to watch people, see the different types and how they interacted. Analyze them a little and guess what made them tick. There were three waitresses circling the room, all very pretty and in their early to late twenties. The crowd was a bit younger than it used to be, too. They were closer to Faith's age now, when they used to be more like Dad's. Or maybe her memories were skewed that way, since she'd been a teenager when she frequently ate here, and everyone had seemed older.

She tipped up her beer and took a long pull. The last

thing she'd expected when she'd bolted from town the week after she graduated high school was to end up back here. Up until two months ago, she thought she'd laid permanent roots in Atlanta. It was a big deal for her, too. Usually she got antsy staying in one place for too long. She'd survived six years in Atlanta, albeit she'd moved seven times. It was one reason she'd hesitated when Jeff mentioned he'd found a great deal on a condo. Her palms had itched when she thought about that long of a commitment to one place, but then he'd wrapped his arms around her and asked her to move in with him, and she'd fallen for it hook, line, and sinker. She wondered if he ever cared, or if he just needed someone to pay half the bills.

Now she needed a new life plan, and coming back to the tiny town she grew up in felt like going backward instead of moving forward. But she supposed coming here, facing Daddy's picture and the pull of memories, was step one of changing her run, hide, and avoid defense mechanism. While there was an edge of sorrow, she liked being here, thinking of the good memories with Dad. It was more empowering than she thought it'd be. Step two was going to take some serious buildup, but she thought if she faced her past and got over the fears she still struggled to let go of, she could finish the healing process and truly move on with her future.

The internship in Charlotte was a one-year program. She was hoping to break her pattern and find a place to live, with a solid career to follow—no more running when life got hard. *Maybe I'll even find someone who wants to settle down with me for real.*

The door of the Rusty Anchor swung open, automatically drawing her attention, and in walked Connor. One of the waitresses greeted him with a smile and he grinned right back. They exchanged a few words—Faith couldn't hear them, but she supposed there was purring from her and a cheesy pickup line from him. He started toward the bar, and Faith wished she had a menu to duck behind.

His gaze moved across the room and she dropped her head, hoping he wouldn't notice her, and making sure he at least didn't think she was staring at him. He headed straight to the bar and nodded at the waitress there, who leaned over the bar and smiled at him. Their exchange was different. More familiar.

Not like I didn't know he was that way with every girl. Still, there was a twinge of disappointment. *Why am I always so attracted to players?*

The waitress brought her food, which at least blocked her view of Connor. Plus, fries, so bonus points. The second she moved, though, Connor was not only in Faith's line of sight, but also coming toward her. He settled in the seat on the other side of the small circular table. "Hey, Blondie. You never called."

"I'm sure you've been sitting waiting by the phone, too."

He reached across and snagged one of her fries.

"Haven't you heard of personal boundaries?"

"Overrated." He signaled the waitress who'd just brought the food and gestured to Faith. "I'll have what she's having. Except just water to drink."

"Sure thing," the waitress said, beaming at him.

When she was gone, Connor nudged Faith's foot with his. "Good guess, figuring I'd be here."

"I did not..." Faith clenched her jaw, knowing the less she gave him, the less he could send back at her. "There are a lot of other open tables. Maybe you and your ego would be more comfortable at one of them."

Connor leaned back, hooking his fingers behind his head. "Naw. I'm good here."

Faith picked up the glass ketchup bottle and shook it, but the red paste remained inside. She picked up a butter knife to try to get some out, but Connor reached over and took the bottle.

"Here. Haven't you ever heard of the magic fifty-seven bang?" He waggled his eyebrows, then pounded the bottle over the fifty-seven on the glass and a puddle of ketchup landed on her plate.

"Thanks," she begrudgingly said. "That's the only bang you'll be getting over here, by the way, so you might want to put your efforts toward one of the waitresses."

"Not interested."

"Right. Because you already slept with all of them."

"I have not."

"So the girl behind the bar...?"

Connor pressed his lips together. "That's different. She was my girlfriend for a while when I was in the academy. We're just friends now."

Well, at least he hadn't straight-up denied it. "How long did you date?"

"Oh, no. I'm not going into exes, unless you're willing to offer up stories of yours first."

Since hers were all examples in dating disasters and the last one still stung, there was no way that was happening. "Fine. Right now, we'll just focus on who we've slept with in this room." Faith made a big show of looking around. "Okay, that's no one for me." She tilted her head toward the waitress who'd greeted him and raised her eyebrows.

He exhaled. "Once. Months ago. I come here all the time, and it's a small town. Why's it matter to you?"

"It doesn't. I'm simply making a point. I'm not interested in being another in your long line of women. Now I've saved you several hours and skeezy lines you can use on someone else. You're welcome."

Two creases formed between his eyebrows. "My lines are not skeezy." He actually looked hurt—or maybe he was only pretending. Either way, she wondered if she'd been too harsh.

Then again, she needed to be harsh. With him and herself. Because once you found your boyfriend with someone else's legs wrapped around him, it was too late to avoid being hurt.

Faith shrugged and tossed another fry in her mouth.

"Besides, I didn't come over here to hit on you," Connor said. "You just looked lonely sitting all alone, and I thought I'd come keep you company. Be friendly and the like. I'm not as diabolical as you think."

Their waitress came over and sat Connor's drink in front of him. "Your food will be right up," she said, batting her eyes at him. "And if you need anything else, let me know."

Once they were alone again, Connor folded his forearms on the table and leaned in. "For the record, I haven't slept with her."

"You'll forgive me if I figure most everything out of your mouth is bullshit."

"Well, with you, I figure it's going to be all bitchiness."

For a moment, they glared at each other. Then the waitress interrupted the stare-down by placing a beer in front of Connor.

"I only ordered the water," he said, glancing up at her.

"Oops. Must've been for my other customer. Why don't you just go ahead and take it while I get it all sorted out." She flashed Connor a flirtatious smile. "Sorry, it's only my second day and I'm still getting the hang of things."

As soon as the waitress was gone, Faith raised an eyebrow at Connor.

"Don't say it," he said.

She sat back in her chair. "I don't think I have to."

• • •

Connor sat at the bar, where the waitress had set his food and a napkin with her name and number on it. He'd left the free beer that had cost him quite a bit as far as Faith was concerned and had moved to one of the bar stools. Irritation coursed through his veins and he gripped the glass in his hand tighter. How dare Faith make him feel bad because women liked him and he liked them back. And what business was it of hers who he'd slept with?

She'd looked so smug when that waitress announced she'd only worked here for two days, and he could see her thoughts all over her face. Like he actually couldn't control who he slept with.

He shouldn't have gone over there in the first place. After the talk with Kaleb this morning, he'd decided to keep his distance from Faith, sure that'd be all it'd take to get her out of his head. But then she'd been sitting there alone, and he thought it'd be rude not to go talk to her. It was like he couldn't help flirting with her once he was next to her, though, his attraction speaking louder than his brain. And then he'd somehow gotten pulled into a fight that got way out of control, past their usual banter and into contempt.

Well, he was definitely cured of his interest in Kaleb's little sister now. Give him a woman who wouldn't make him feel like shit. He doubted he could come back from the angry exchange they'd had anyway—he shouldn't have lost it like that, telling her he expected bitchiness, regardless of what she'd said first. Now she was sitting over at her table, pretending he didn't exist as she hurriedly ate her food, and he was sitting at the bar, doing the same thing.

I bet it'd piss her off if I flirted with the waitress. If she's gonna accuse me of being with them all, I might as well have the benefit of being guilty of it. He caught the dark-haired girl's attention and she rushed over—leaving her other table in the lurch from the looks of it.

He cast one glance at Faith and she ducked her head as if she hadn't been watching. That was another annoying thing.

He could see the way she looked at him. Why pretend she wasn't as attracted as he was?

It doesn't matter, because she's not an option anyway.

Only now that the waitress was here, blinking her eyes at him, he found he didn't want to piss off Faith. For one thing, he'd see her all the time, and he didn't want things to be weird every time he went over to Kaleb's. And he swore he could suddenly feel the picture of Faith's dad staring at him, another reminder of why he didn't want to hurt Faith, even if she didn't give a damn about him.

The waitress put her hand on his arm. "Did you need something, sugar?"

"Yeah, that woman I was sitting with? Add her meal to my bill, will you? And go ahead and bring it to me as soon as you get a chance. Please."

"And that's it?" the girl asked, a hopeful glint in her eye.

She was plenty pretty, but he wasn't even interested enough to keep her number as a just in case. "That's it."

Chapter Four

"Aren't there pregnant lady labor laws or something?" Faith asked as she took one of the rakes and a small spade shovel from Anna.

"In order to get a good location at the festival for my pottery booth, I basically had to sell my soul to Mrs. Lowery. I signed up to head the park cleanup and decorating committee and promised to make three pies for the pie toss. I even signed up Kaleb for a couple things, just to make sure I was on her good side."

"That woman's a total slave driver. I remember when she was in charge of the town pageant and made us practice until we were in danger of passing out." Faith had spent the last few days helping Anna get the baby's room ready, but she said she couldn't put off cleaning up the park any longer.

Anna leaned her rake against the car and opened the door to get Ella out of her seat. "Remember to stick close," she said, and Ella wiggled down and took off running toward the gazebo. They'd had to wait until after her nap was over to avoid meltdown, so the sun was already low in the sky, sunset only a few hours away. At least it wouldn't be too hot.

"There you are!" Mrs. Lowery strode toward them, arms swinging and an expression on her face that said she was on a mission. "I was starting to think I'd have to do everything myself." Wanting to take the pressure off Anna, Faith opened her mouth to assure the older woman that she didn't need to worry, but Mrs. Lowery pinned her with a look that made her want to run in the direction Ella had gone. "Are you back in town now?"

"Um. For a little while."

"Great. After this area is cleaned up, flowers will need to be planted. Go to Sprouts and ask them for the mums and daisies. Make sure to spread them out around the gazebo so that you can see flowers no matter where you're at."

"But I—"

"Apparently a few of the town's tents have holes in them, so I've got to see just how bad they are, and if we're going to need to place a rush order for more." Mrs. Lowery sighed a martyr's sigh. "If I don't take care of things, no one else will." She shook her head and then was off, arms swinging again.

"Welcome to the cleanup and decorating committee," Anna said with a smile.

Faith slid on a pair of gardening gloves. "I knew I should've gone into Charlotte to look for an apartment today," she joked, though she was glad she could help Anna out. Especially when she saw just how messy Magnolia Park was—from the looks of it, no one had taken care of it in a while.

They got to work, raking leaves and pulling weeds. "Mrs. Lowery really expects you to do this all on your own?" Faith asked as she tugged on a stubborn dandelion.

"Oh, there's a group of us, but everyone keeps flaking out, claiming work or family obligations, and since I'm lucky enough to be the leader of the group, I get all the phone calls with constant reminders of how I only get a discount on a booth *if* I do my assignment." Anna wiped her forearm across her brow. "Ella, get down. Now."

Ella was halfway up the railing of the gazebo, one leg over the edge. She froze in place at her mom's voice. Faith wasn't sure if all nearly three-year-old kids loved danger, or if her niece was just some kind of toddler daredevil. The girl couldn't seem to sit still, and the more dangerous the task, the more she was drawn to it. Between keeping an eye on her and all the work, an hour passed in a heartbeat, and they still had a long way to go.

Faith hoped Mrs. Lowery didn't think the flowers were going to get planted today. She couldn't help noticing the gazebo looked pretty beat-up, too, shingles missing, the lattice coming apart, and a plank sticking up that Ella had tripped on at least three times. A ladder was propped on the side, too, which Ella took as a challenge, so Anna eventually had to lay it flat on the ground to keep her from climbing it.

With nothing but work to focus on, Faith's thoughts drifted, and one thing kept coming to mind, even though she tried to stop it. More like one person. She hadn't seen Connor since he'd paid for her dinner at the Rusty Anchor. She still couldn't believe he'd done that after everything she'd said to him. It'd left her with an unresolved nagging feeling, and she told herself that was all it was. That she was glad he'd stopped being so inescapable.

But since she had to keep telling herself over and over again, she was having a hard time convincing herself it was completely true.

• • •

Connor had kept busy the past few days, staying at the station until late. Domestic dispute and abuse calls always got to him, and Tuesday was the third time he'd gone to Hal and Erica Corbett's house in the past six months. The first call had been more than a year ago, and he'd hoped ever since that she'd take out a protective order and press charges. So he'd spent all day yesterday and today making calls, checking in with the prosecutor, trying to ensure Mr. Corbett finally got what was coming to him.

The phone on his desk rang and he picked up. "Officer Maguire."

Sullivan was on the other end, and when he hesitated, Connor knew it'd be bad news. "Sorry, man. We couldn't hold Hal Corbett any longer. We might be able to give him thirty to sixty days for resisting arrest, but it'll have a hard time sticking, and without Erica..."

Connor pinched the bridge of his nose. "I know." Damn, did he know. No matter how many people he had helped, it came down to her being willing to press charges. "Thanks for the call." He hung up and released a string of swearwords.

Kaleb glanced up from his desk. "Mrs. Corbett isn't pressing charges, is she?"

Connor gritted his teeth and shook his head. "He beat the shit out of her this time. And now he'll go home and do it all over again. I thought I'd finally gotten through." His failure sat like a cold, hard lump in his gut.

"You did everything you could. She still loves him for some reason. She thinks jail would be too harsh; I could tell when we talked to her."

The things people got away with in the name of love. Yet another reason to avoid it. "She thinks he'll change, too, but she's going to be calling us again. Or maybe he won't even allow that next time. Maybe I can convince the boss to put an extra patrol unit in that neighborhood—Hal should at least know we'll check in. I'm personally stopping by tomorrow to make sure Erica doesn't have any fresh bruises."

Kaleb came around Connor's desk and sat on the edge. "You're too close, and you're gonna get yourself in trouble." Connor opened his mouth to argue, but Kaleb put a hand on his shoulder and said, "But if you ignore this warning, like I know you're going to, you sure as hell better take me along so I can make sure things don't get out of control."

That was the blessing and curse of having a partner who knew you too well. He nodded. That much he could do.

"Anna called to remind me that the gazebo still needs fixing."

Connor picked up the paperwork he'd filled out and crumpled it into a tight ball. He launched it into the nearby trashcan, the nice shot doing nothing to take away the thickness in his lungs. He just wanted to go home, but Anna had signed Kaleb up for gazebo duty and asked Connor if he'd help, too. Mrs. Lowery had even cornered him in the coffee shop yesterday to remind him that he'd promised to help. "Maybe hammering something will make me feel better."

After a quick stop at his place to pick up tools, they headed to Magnolia Park. The sun was just about down, but with the lights shining on the gazebo, he could make out Anna, Faith, and Ella. Connor rubbed a finger across his bottom lip. Yes, he'd been busy, but he'd also been avoiding Faith. After the restaurant the other night, he had no idea how their next meeting would go, and he wasn't sure he wanted Kaleb witnessing it.

Too late now. He got out of the car and took off his collared shirt, leaving him in a plain white tank top. As they walked toward the girls, he contemplated how to deal with Faith. Indifference? Act like nothing had changed? Give up flirting with her? Try to be friends?

Ella came running toward them, a streak of pink and curls. She wrapped herself around Kaleb's leg. After he bent down to kiss her forehead, she bounced over to Connor.

He scooped her up and tossed her in the air. She squealed and erupted in giggles. She gave him a sticky kiss on the cheek—her hands were sticky as well, purple with grass stuck to them—then she wiggled down and took off back toward her mom.

Kaleb walked over to Anna, and Faith straightened, glancing Connor's way. Her blond hair was pulled into a high ponytail, dirt was smudged across her cheek, and she was wearing a red tank top and tiny jean shorts that showed off her legs. His heart gave a hard thump and he decided it'd be a shame to totally give up flirting with her. So he winked. "Hey, Blondie. How've you been?"

She crossed her arms in a way that emphasized her cleavage. "Fine." Her gaze dropped to the ground for a moment and then came back up to him. "Actually, I feel bad about the other night."

"I think we both said some things we didn't mean."

She twisted the handle of the rake in her hands. "And I also wanted to say thanks…for dinner. You didn't need to pay for my food."

"Least I could do after acting like a jerk."

Her eyebrows shot up, the surprise clear on her features. It only lasted a second before she narrowed her eyes at him. "It won't change my mind about…" She lowered her voice. "You know."

"Okay," he said, keeping his voice and face carefully neutral. Then he walked up the rickety stairs of the gazebo and went to work, hammering down loose boards. Kaleb started on the outside, but after about twenty minutes, Ella started crying for him and throwing tantrums when he didn't pick her up.

"Go home," Faith said to Anna. "I've almost tackled this mess of weeds, so I'll work for a little longer. I don't mind."

Anna asked if she was sure, and when Faith nodded, she picked up Ella. But she was still crying for her dad, arms stretched toward him, trying to break free from her obviously tired mom.

Connor looked through the archway to Kaleb. "You should go, too. I got this. Go be with your family."

Kaleb sighed and then handed the hammer through to him. "Thanks. I owe you." He glanced at Faith.

"I'll take her home when we're done."

Kaleb's eyes narrowed.

"Dude, I got your message the other day, loud and clear," he said, keeping his voice low. "I'll just give her a ride. Besides, she hates me, remember?"

Faith straightened and must've realized what was going on. She waved Kaleb on. "Go ahead. I'd rather get as much done as possible than have Mrs. Lowery calling Anna all the time."

He muttered a thanks and rushed over to the van to help Anna get Ella buckled in. For a while, it was quiet, only the sound of the occasional car, his hammer, or the scrape of Faith's rake. He'd smashed his fingers a couple times, thanks to Faith bending over to tug at a weed.

When she came up the stairs, her ponytail was tilted to one side, several strands of hair coming loose around her face. "I'm surprised Mrs. Lowery let this thing get so run-down. If she wants it all picturesque-looking for the festival, it needs some major repairs."

"That storm last year around hurricane season beat it up pretty bad. But it could always be worse. Some guy ran his boat into one of the pier gazebos on Sherrills Ford's side of the lake last week. Totally destroyed it."

"He just ran into it? How do you not see something like that coming?"

"My guess? Lots of alcohol."

"Probably a good guess." She dropped her gloves and rake on one of the benches and propped an elbow on the ledge, looking out toward Lake Norman. Connor put away his tools and went to join her. The urge to put his hand on her back was strong, so he shoved his hands in his pockets.

Clouds obscured the moon, leaving only the dim glow from the nearby lampposts. Then little sparks of light flashed through the darkness, a glow here and there. More and more lightning bugs showed up, dotting the blackness like hundreds of stars hovering just above the ground.

"I missed lightning bugs when I was in Atlanta," she said, looking around at the glittering insects, her eyes wide. "I'd see one here and there, but nothing like this." One corner of her mouth turned up. "I used to be scared of the dark, so Kaleb would fill a jar with them every night for me. I feel kinda bad for all the poor little bugs who died trying to light my room." She glanced at him, seemed to remember she didn't talk to him like that usually, and the revelry disappeared from her features.

He nudged her with his elbow. "You don't have to be so guarded around me. You can let go a little."

"And have you use it against me?" Faith shook her head.

"True. Wait until the newspaper gets ahold of the story about the girl who killed lightning bugs. In fact, I'd better take you in right now." He placed his hand over the handcuffs on his belt.

She arched her eyebrows and sucked her bottom lip between her teeth, and his mind shot right to the gutter. He cleared his throat. "You started that one."

Her mouth dropped open. "I didn't say anything!"

"Sweetheart, your eyes said it all." He lowered his hand from his cuffs and jerked his chin out toward the darkness lit with twinkling bug butts. "Now, behave, will you? I'm trying to watch bugs catch a mate. See if I can't get some tips."

"Hell, make your ass glow, and I might take back everything I've said about you."

Desire swirled through him. If he thought he could get away with it, he'd pull her to him and kiss that sassy mouth of hers. But he was slowly figuring out that she was attracted to confidence, but also scared off by it. And then there was the fact that he wasn't supposed to be thinking about kissing her. He remembered the look Kaleb had given him and tried to rein himself in. Friends. Without benefits.

But he couldn't help smiling, because she obviously didn't hate him half as much as she claimed.

• • •

Faith was trying not to smile, but she was totally failing. Maybe it was the lightning bugs, or the perfect fall evening, or maybe it was the hot, obnoxious, yet irresistible cop standing next to her. She meant what she'd said earlier—things had gotten out of control at the Rusty Anchor, and she'd felt bad about it. Especially when, after waiting *forever* for her check, the waitress had told her, "The hot guy who was sitting with you earlier paid it already." She'd looked all put out about it, too, which made Faith think he didn't hit on the one waitress he hadn't slept with yet.

When a few days passed without seeing him, she wondered if he was purposely avoiding her. She'd told herself it was for the best—that she had plans to make and bigger things to worry about. But standing out here, muscles fatigued from hours of landscaping work, bugs glittering around them, her cares melted away. Didn't mean she wasn't going to be cautious with the guy next to her. She supposed they could be friends, though. If only he couldn't read her thoughts so easily—she'd have to work on her poker face.

Connor leaned down beside her, his massive bare arms

folded across the railing. He peered off in the distance, and suddenly he seemed to be a hundred miles away. The muscles in his jaw tensed and his brow creased, leading her to believe it wasn't a happy place.

"So, Miss Psychiatry Major, tell me something."

"Psychology, actually," Faith said. "And I'll do my best." He stared at her for a beat—happened most anytime she pointed out there was a difference. "It's more figuring out why people do what they do and counseling than the medical side of physical exams and prescribing medication. I hope to be a counselor someday." She waved her hand, wishing she hadn't bothered explaining. "Anyway, what's your question?"

He gripped the railing, his eyes glued to the lake. "Why would a woman stay with a man who beats her?"

The question slammed her in the gut—of all the things he could ask, she hadn't expected that. The set of his jaw and the hardness around his eyes told her it was a serious question. "There are a lot of reasons, which I know is a crappy answer, but it's the truth. It could be she has a history of being treated badly, so she's used to it or has accepted that as standard. Or she feels a false sense of security or thinks she has too much to lose. Low self-esteem is a big reason, pretty much at the base of all those reasons. Sometimes she starts out with it, and sometimes the guy's stripped her of it." Faith shot him a sidelong glance. "I'm assuming you have a reason for asking."

"Got a case," he said, but there was so much more behind the words. His mask dropped for a moment, a glimmer of a vulnerable person underneath, before it ascended once again. "Anyway. I know what the clinical answers are. Just wondered if you had a different take."

As if she couldn't help herself, she placed her hand over his. "I'd like to say I could find the one reason and cure them all of it. But knowing something and really knowing it—like when we're in that irrational state of being threatened or when love is thrown into the mix—isn't easy. That's the thing about humans. We're all messed up in one way or another."

He turned his eyes on her, his face half-light and half-shadowed. She swallowed and tried to tell her fluttering heart to knock it off. "I guess that's why they pay you the big bucks," he said.

"Right now they pay me nothing," she said with a laugh.

"Well, you're worth every penny." Connor turned his palm up and curled his fingers around her hand, his skin warm compared to the cool night air. "So. Are we friends again?"

"'Again' is a strong word," she joked. "But yes. I suppose we're *friends.*"

"Who occasionally…" He dragged his slightly calloused thumb across the inside of her wrist and her pulse underneath the thin skin quickened in response. "Watch fireflies together."

She shook her head but couldn't help smiling. "Yes. That type of friends."

A devastatingly handsome smile curved his lips. "I guess we'd better go before I screw it up, then. And before my dog decides to tear apart something—she gets destructive when I leave her for too long."

They gathered up the tools and put them in the police cruiser. "I suppose I should make you ride in the back," Connor said with a grin. "That way you can't attack me while I'm trying to drive."

"Remember the not-screwing-it-up thing? You're walking a fine line."

His grin only widened. He opened the passenger door for her and she climbed inside. It was a little weird to be riding in a police vehicle. And she couldn't not think about Daddy in here, too, sitting in the spot Kaleb usually did. Or the one Connor was climbing into.

"You okay?" Connor asked, and she forced herself to

shake off memories of the cruiser parked in the driveway. How she'd see it out there and know her dad was home. How one day it hadn't been there anymore.

"Just tired from all the landscaping."

For the first time since she'd met him, Connor was quiet, not talking as they rode the short distance to Kaleb's. She grabbed for the door handle. "Thanks for the ride. I'm sure I'll see you later."

"If you want to make it sooner rather than later, tomorrow's a swim instead of run day. Why don't you meet me at the lake at six and we'll see if you can keep up?"

"Six? In the morning? I'll be in bed. Sleeping," she added before he took it as an invitation or chance to say something dirty. "But you have fun."

Connor tipped his head at her. "Night, Blondie."

"Good night, Big and Beefy."

He laughed, the edges of his eyes crinkling, and her stomach flip-flopped. Definitely a sign that it was time to put some space between them.

As she walked up the sidewalk, she caught sight of more twinkling lightning bugs. There were few things in life you could bottle and hold onto. Even the glow of the insects wouldn't last. But right now, she wanted to bottle the carefree, happy sensation in her chest before the apprehension creeping in on the edges could take it away.

Being around Connor felt slightly reckless in a delicious way she craved despite knowing the danger, which made her worry she hadn't learned anything from her past relationships.

Still, there was something different about Connor—something he worked to hide—and the curious part of her wanted to dig deeper and figure out what had happened to him to make that split second of vulnerability cross his features.

Chapter Five

Faith was surprised to see Connor in the park, hammering away on the gazebo, his dog pacing the ground around him. She supposed it only made sense that he was off if Kaleb was, since they were partners, but she definitely hadn't expected him to be spending his day off this way.

Anna was going to come to help finish up the landscaping, too, but she'd looked exhausted, so Faith told her she could take care of the flowers. She'd picked them up from Sprouts, just like Mrs. Lowery had ordered. Balancing the boxes, she made her way across the grassy area. Connor was in faded jeans and a navy shirt that stretched across his chest as he placed a pale plank of wood in place. A tall, scrawny guy with dusty-brown hair was on the inside, the constant pounding of his hammer cutting through the quiet morning.

"What do you think, Pen?" Connor asked, surveying the plank he was holding in place. "Does it look straight?"

Penny wagged her tail, then turned to Faith and padded over. Faith set down the boxes of flowers so she could pet her, trying not to think about how adorable it was that Connor talked to his dog.

He pounded a couple of nails in place and then jumped down. The other guy descended the steps of the gazebo.

"Looks like Mrs. Lowery has been busy gathering more victims," Faith said.

"She's my grandma," the tall guy said and Faith clamped her lips shut, not sure how to respond to that. Oops.

Connor covered his smile with his hand. "Sullivan, this is Faith. Kaleb's very little sister. Faith, Garth Sullivan."

Faith started to put the name with the family. Lowery and Sullivan. "I think I went to school with your sister. Caroline?"

He nodded.

"How is she these days?"

"Fine." Apparently Garth wasn't much of a talker. Or maybe she'd offended him. His phone chirped with a text and he looked at the screen. "Speaking of my grandma, looks like she needs me to meet her at the hardware store. I'll be back in a few." He pocketed his phone and headed off toward a beat-up white pickup, and Faith really hoped he wasn't going to share their whole exchange with Mrs. Lowery. If he wanted to spread the word that she was here and doing her flower duty, though, that'd be great.

When Faith glanced at Connor, he shook his head. "Making fun of his grandma."

"Shut it." Faith shoved him, which ended up being like shoving a wall—he could've at least humored her and faked a wobble. "And don't think I didn't notice the *very little*." She moved to start digging holes for the flowers so she wouldn't do something stupid like start flirting with Connor. Penny sniffed around the ground next to her for a while before taking off after a grasshopper.

The spade, gloves, and scent of damp earth reminded her of Mom. She used to love gardening, and was always out digging in the soil and watering her plants. Then, after Dad died, she just stopped, always in her room, refusing to go out. Faith had called Mom yesterday and tried to convince her to come down and visit—it'd been almost a year since they'd seen each other—but she'd claimed she was too busy taking care of Grandma and Grandpa to get away. She told Faith that she could, of course, come visit them, though.

Connor's hammering broke through and for a moment she focused on each swing of his hammer, the echo in the air. "If you had the day off, why were you up at six a.m. to swim?"

He finished pounding in the nail he was working on. "Why not?"

"I can think of fifty reasons at least, number one being more sleep."

Connor shrugged. "Habit, I guess. Plus, Mrs. Lowery sent out a reminder that the gazebo needed to be done ASAP so it'd be ready for the pie toss. The plan is for the guys at the station to be the *victims*. You know how Sullivan's grandma can be." He flashed her a mocking grin.

"I should've known better. Say a bad word about anyone in this town, and odds are someone's related to her." Faith patted the damp earth around the orange mums she'd set in the ground. It seemed like a lot of work to plant flowers right in time for them to die a month or two later, but she knew better than to mention that to Mrs. Lowery.

"Don't worry. Sullivan was complaining earlier about how he'd gotten roped into it." Connor took a couple steps up the ladder. "So, after you enjoyed your sleeping in, did you go for a run?"

Faith wondered if she could count it as a run, since she'd walked most of it and swore through the running parts. "Yeah. I'm trying to get ready for the Fallen Officer 5K, but thanks to how hectic my last semester of school was, I'm out of shape."

Connor glanced down at her, one eyebrow quirking

higher than the other. "Your shape looks fine to me." She shook her head, trying to keep a smile off her lips as she dug another hole. "If you want, though, I can train with you."

"Uh, no thanks. I'm not running next to you."

"Why not?"

"Because you wake up at the butt crack of dawn to exercise and look like you live at a gym. I'll do what I can to get ready for the race in the next few weeks and call it a success if I'm not the very last person crossing the line."

"With my help, you wouldn't be. And I'm running it, too. We could do it together. I'll cheer you on the whole time."

"I'm going to stick with my 'no thanks' answer." Just thinking about running next to him made her want to skip the race altogether. But the event was about more than her and the Muppet-flail run she'd probably be doing by the end. "I'll see you at the finish line."

"Suit yourself." Connor tucked a bundle of shingles under his arm and climbed up the ladder.

"Are you sure that roof can even hold you?"

"Only one way to find out." The ladder rattled as he neared the top, and she jumped up to hold it steady, not wanting to witness him tumble down, even if a knock on the head might be good for his inflated ego. Penny came over as if she were going to help.

"He's a little bit crazy, you know," Faith said to the dog, and Penny gave a happy bark, which Faith took to mean she totally agreed.

Once Connor was on the roof, hammering away on the shingles, she returned to her flower planting. She'd made it all the way around the gazebo by the time Grant came back, a can of paint in each hand, his grandma by his side.

Connor was just climbing down from the roof, his hammer in the front pocket of his jeans. Not that she was checking out that area or anything.

"Faith," Mrs. Lowery said brightly, a huge smile curving her lips, and she thought, *Yes! Grant didn't rat me out.* "I'm so happy you volunteered to help."

So many things she wanted to say to that, but she bit her tongue. She could practically feel Connor grinning behind her as he gave her elbow a light pinch. "She's a giver, our Faith."

Faith jerked her arm back, catching Connor in the gut, and his fingers wrapped around her biceps, holding her in place as his low laugh sounded in her ear.

Mrs. Lowery didn't seem to notice. "I'm sure between you, Grant, and Officer Maguire, you'll have no trouble getting that gazebo looking good as new." She handed a heavy plastic bag over to Faith. "Here are the paint supplies. I hear it might rain tomorrow, and we're going to need at least two coats, so why don't we see if we can get the first coat done today."

With that, Mrs. Lowery took off, leaving Faith standing with the bag of paintbrushes, rollers, and mixing trays, Connor still holding onto one of her arms. Faith liked how she'd worded it as *we*, even thought it was clearly a *you*. Give that woman an inch, and soon you're spending all of your free time cleaning up Magnolia Park.

Connor released her arm and took the bag from her. He lifted a roller out of it and then handed her one, his fingers wrapping around hers. Mischief flickered in his eyes. "I'm so happy you volunteered to help, too."

• • •

Connor felt wet against his neck.

"Oops," Faith said, but she was grinning, leading him to believe she wasn't all that sorry about the paint that'd dripped onto him. She was up on the ladder, arm stretched above her, a strip of skin showing between her pants and shirt. He ducked as another glob dripped off her roller, moving just in time to keep from being hit.

"That's why I should be on the ladder."

"No, you're tall as it is. Which is why *I* should be on the ladder. But I need some more paint."

Sullivan had gone to get dinner, but he was taking forever, which wasn't necessarily a bad thing. It was pretty impressive how much the three of them had gotten done, but his arms were beginning to ache—not that he'd ever admit it.

Faith ran her roller through the paint, and he lowered his arm, watching the motion. Letting her claim the ladder made it easier to steal glances when she was focused on the work in front of her. White paint splattered her hair and face. "You've got some on your cheek," he said, reaching forward to wipe it for her. Only it smudged more than took it off, and he apparently had paint on his hand.

She gasped. "You put more on, I felt it! Oh, you asked for it." Before he could protest, she ran the roller down his arm. He lunged for her, catching her around the waist, and she let out a cute little squeal. He wiped his paint-coated arm across her.

After that, paint started flying, a stripe here and there, until they were both covered in it. Her chest rose and fell with her breaths as she circled him, roller out, jabbing it like a sword.

When Sullivan showed up, two brown paper bags in his hands, his eyes widened as he took in the scene.

Connor slowly set down his roller and held up his hands. "I give up. I'm too hungry to fight you anymore."

"Wimp."

He grabbed her hand and yanked her to him, the wet roller smashing between them. "What was that?"

She laughed, that fiery spark in her eyes. "Nothing." When she wiggled against him, his breath went shallow and blood rushed through his veins. He could feel the paint soaking in, too, but with her this close, he wasn't so much worried about that.

"Looks like Kaleb came to help," Sullivan said, and Connor quickly dropped his hold on Faith, the roller falling to the grass between them. *Shit.* If his partner saw that, he'd have a fit, and it was only a bit of innocent flirting.

With not-so-innocent thoughts mixed in.

By the time Kaleb made it over, they were digging into their burgers, and Connor had made sure there was plenty of space between him and Faith, even though he was still thinking about her laugh and the lightness in his chest whenever she was around. He'd thought he'd do his time here for the town, but he'd never expected how much fun it'd be.

Penny had been off by the lake, but now that there was food, she was down at his feet whimpering. He tossed her the second patty from his burger, trying not to look like he was listening to Kaleb and Faith's conversation.

"...realize this was where you were all day," Kaleb said.

"I'm trying to help out," Faith said. "Well, more like I've been ordered to, but it wasn't so bad. I don't think I can lift my hands over my head anymore, though, and Anna's supposed to show me the pottery she's putting on display." She finished off her burger, handed her painting supplies to her brother, and gathered up the boxes from the flowers she'd planted earlier.

Kaleb started on the far side of the gazebo, and Connor tossed Penny the rest of his food. He supposed they might as well finish today if they could. He was pouring more paint in the tray when Faith walked past him. She put her hand on his arm and he froze in place, afraid to move because she might let go and afraid not to because her brother might see.

"I hate to be the one to tell you this, Hotshot, but it looks like you're going gray."

Connor ran a hand through his hair, sure it was coated in white. "Cop work I can handle, but painting with you is stressful."

She smiled, a groove forming in the corner of her cheek. Then she walked on, and he had to force himself to turn toward the gazebo instead of watching her walk away like he would've if her brother wasn't a few yards back, probably paying close attention to their interaction.

. . .

Anna and Faith walked across the backyard to the toolshed Kaleb had converted to a pottery studio for his wife. Anna undid the deadbolt on the door. "Can't risk Ella getting in here without me. She'd have the place destroyed in two minutes flat."

They'd had to set her up in front of *Sleeping Beauty* with a cup of chocolate milk so Anna could finally show Faith the studio she'd been telling her all about. Anna flicked on the lights, illuminating the plates, vases, and bowls in various colors. A potter's wheel sat in the middle. She put her hands on her stomach. "With this thing in the way, it's been a while since I threw any clay."

"Clay throwing. Sounds violent."

Anna laughed and described the pottery-making process, from shaping the clay on the wheel to glazing and firing. Her eyes lit up as she talked about it, so Faith asked her more questions, listening as she went into minerals and how they changed the colors, and the different kinds of firing processes. "I've always wanted to do a show, and I'm a little nervous for my first one at the festival, but I'm also really excited. Hopefully I can at least make enough money to justify what I spent on supplies."

"It's going to be great." Faith tucked her damp hair behind her ear. It'd taken a lot of shampoo and soap to scrub off the paint, and thanks to her and Connor's paint fight, she was pretty sure she'd still find random splotches of the stuff for the next week.

"What's the smile for?" Anna asked and Faith jerked up her head, feeling like she'd been caught.

"I was just thinking it's cool that you have a hobby you're so passionate about."

Anna narrowed her eyes like she didn't quite buy it, but she let it go. "It's nice to have something that's all mine. Being a mom is great, and I love it, but at the end of the day there's nothing more relaxing than getting my hands on some clay and watching it take shape. I'm still figuring out a few tricks with the firing cycle and glazes. I'm thinking I'll even try crystals after I recover from having Junior." She rubbed her stomach again and then picked up a large green-and-bronze plate. "This one's my favorite. Well, one of my favorites."

Faith carefully took it from her, admiring the colors and the smooth line of the rim. "Everyone needs a hobby they can use to escape the world for a while. I'm still trying to figure out mine." She handed the plate back and Anna set it in place again.

"So, you and Connor just painted together all day? And you somehow ended up covered in it?"

Apparently she wasn't actually letting it go. "Grant Sullivan was there, too. For most of it, anyway."

Anna arched her eyebrow. "I feel like there're a lot of things you're not saying. I get a couple paint splatters, but what you had going on looked like something…more. And when Kaleb called to check in, he was all put out about how the two of you were acting when he showed up."

Faith was afraid to say too much, because she was trying to convince herself she wasn't still thinking about how fun today had been. "At first I thought Connor was a total jerk, but he does have some redeeming qualities." Like how he spent his entire day helping out on a town project and brought his dog. And he was kind of funny. Over-the-top flirty but a good sport. "We've agreed to be friends. But that's it. He's a player *and* a cop, which means I'm not interested."

"Honey, every woman with eyes is interested in that man. I know he might come off rough at first, but he's got a good heart. He's been so good to Kaleb, and he's great with Ella. I've been hoping he'd find a cute girl and settle down."

"He's not the settling-down type, Anna. He's the type to break hearts." Faith picked up a pink vase and studied it before cautiously setting it back down. She was paranoid she was going to tip something over and send everything crashing to the ground. "And if he's so great, why would Kaleb care if I spent time with him?"

"Well…he doesn't see the potential like I do. Plus, I saw the sparks between you two when he came to dinner. I think if anyone could tame him, it'd be you."

"I'm not interested in taming anyone. Or in being someone's one-night stand." Faith took a ceramic fish off the shelf. It was blue with a yellow tail.

"I made that when I found out I was having a boy."

For some reason, it made Faith want to go fishing. Maybe she'd see if Paul or Brynn was up for it. Funny how she used to think it was lame when she had to go all the time, but now she missed it. Not just it, but how life was back then—Dad out on the water with them, laughing and competing with the rest of the guys for who could catch the most fish. "Makes me think of my dad. He'd like it."

"You might as well bring it inside. I keep meaning to so I can put it in the nursery."

Anna locked up the studio and they headed toward the house.

As hard as Faith tried to push it out of her mind, her thoughts moved back to what Anna had said about Connor. The competitive side of her wondered if she could win him over. Figure out what made him tick and make him the type of guy who'd be happy with one woman.

But she'd made the mistake of being flattered by the *He Chose Me!* trick before. Jeff had had a couple of girls after him when they'd first started dating. She'd decided to win him over, and she thought she had. But halfway through last semester, there were times when he wouldn't answer her calls. When she'd brought it up, he'd acted confused and hurt, making her feel like she was the crazy one. She'd even started thinking she was just being overly paranoid. Especially when he asked her to move in with him.

But deep down there was that prickling, not-quite-right sensation. Didn't make it any easier when she walked in on him and another girl. And she'd known right then and there that it hadn't been a one-time thing. It'd taken every ounce of her self-control to stay in Atlanta and take care of all the paperwork to transfer the condo to him instead of driving away like she'd wanted to.

The second Anna opened the door, Ella yelled, "Mommy!" as she dove off a chair onto her mom, who barely caught her in time.

Anna flinched, her hand going to her stomach.

"Come here, bug." Faith held out her hands and Ella leaped onto her. She curled up against her, head on her shoulder, and Faith's heart expanded with love for her niece. She thought of what she'd seen between Kaleb and Anna since she'd been here. Their life was crazy, but they helped each other, and there was no doubt they loved each other. It wasn't like Faith was ready for a family now, but someday she wanted that, which meant finding a guy who'd be serious about it as well. Not to mention a guy with a stable but not dangerous job. Which meant Connor was out.

The plan to find a nice, humble guy who wouldn't cheat on her was on.

Chapter Six

Connor glanced at the clock as he turned onto the road that led to the helicopter-tour office. He was a little early, but he knew if he'd stayed in Cornelius any longer, he would've been too tempted to stop by Kaleb's place to see Faith, while pretending he wasn't there for that reason. For most of the day, she was all he'd thought about. Replaying their time painting the gazebo had kept him from obsessing over his frustration with the Corbett case. Only now he was obsessing about the feisty blonde. He knew he needed to play it cool—he'd already endured a lot of suspicious looks from her brother yesterday. He was trying not to like Faith, but she'd gotten under his skin. When she was around he didn't feel bored anymore. He wanted to take her out. Not just drinks—that wouldn't be long enough.

And now I'm thinking about her again.

Connor pulled his Silverado up in front of the small office, noticing the sign now had ASK ABOUT OUR ADVENTURE TOURS! freshly painted in red under the retouched CHARLOTTE HELICOPTER TOURS lettering. Wes was outside with his fiancée, Dani. Not many of Connor's friends were single anymore—Kaleb was a family man, and Wes was about to be. Maybe that was why he was suddenly feeling the urge to try dating. Not to mention how Mama had taken to asking if he'd found a nice girl to settle down with yet every time he talked to her. Apparently it went against his Italian heritage to not have a giant family—he suspected she might be making that up, though. And last family dinner, she'd so nicely pointed out that he wasn't getting any younger. Since when was thirty old?

Wes nodded at Connor as he got out of the truck. They'd met back in high school, right after Connor's parents had divorced and Mama had rented a place in Huntersville, next door to the Turners. They'd played a lot of basketball in their driveways, and still got together for the occasional game— Dani was a hell of a ball player, too. When Wes told Connor about the business he was trying to get running, he'd offered to help however he could. They'd spent the past couple of months scouting locations and rating the tours, from beginner to extreme adventure.

Dani pulled out a map, spread it across the hood of his truck, and pointed to an area in the Pisgah National Forest. "We're thinking of trying Harper Creek Falls today. It's supposed to be *the* place in North Carolina for people who want the most difficult hiking experience."

Connor leaned over the map and noted the coordinates. "I'll call it in. See where the property lines are and if we need any special permits. If we're clear, we'll go check it out."

A few minutes later, Connor and Wes were in the helicopter, climbing higher and higher. Dani went with them most of the time, but apparently she had a wedding-planning meeting to get to.

"So, you freaking out yet?" Connor asked.

Wes glanced at him, eyebrows drawn together. "I do this

all the time. Why would I freak out?"

"I mean about getting married. You've got what? Five months?"

"Just over three," Wes said. "I'm ready for the wedding to be done with already. Dani's as mellow as they come, but with my family involved... Well, it's becoming bigger than we expected, and I just want to be married. I want to call her my wife, and for everyone to know she's all mine." He banked the helicopter to the west and the city disappeared underneath them, trees taking over the landscape.

"I'm still not sure about the marriage thing. I might be ready to try to date just one, though. See what all the hype is about." The truth was, he had tried it a couple times before. But not for a long time and never to the point he fully let those women into his life.

"No shit, man? You're ready to take off the training wheels and try a relationship?"

Connor slugged Wes's shoulder and they both laughed. "Maybe that should be your next tour. Try dating one girl! More dangerous than rappelling or cliff diving!" He sat back in his seat. He couldn't believe what he was about to say out loud, but he wanted to tell somebody. Wished he were holding a beer while he was doing it, though. "She's different. I can't get her out of my head, and I'm not sure I want to."

"Then go for it."

"It's complicated." Connor glanced out the windshield, focusing on the green. "Even if I could talk her into it... You remember my partner, Kaleb? She's his sister." He couldn't believe he'd said it aloud. But he was thinking about her all the time, and it wasn't like he could talk to Kaleb about it.

"Dude."

"Right? And he knows me too well."

"Which means he's told you to stay the hell away from her."

Connor nodded. "I just don't know if I can."

"If you're serious about the girl, though…"

That was the question. How serious could he be? The thought of a full-blown relationship caused far more nerves than any of the tours he and Wes had gone on. But the thought of giving up on whatever this thing with Faith was made him feel hollow. And he was so damn sick of that emptiness constantly eating away at him. "I don't know. I think I can do things different with her. I'm almost sure."

Wes shook his head. "Good luck, man. All I can say is once you find the right one, it's easy."

Dating was one thing. Talking about "the one" was a different level entirely. The truth was, he'd never wanted that. All those heightened emotions… Too many bad memories haunted him. What if he was too much like his dad to make it work? He'd rather be alone than turn into him.

"There it is," Wes said, pulling him out of his thoughts. "We touch down in that open meadow, then hike up to the falls."

Adrenaline coursed through Connor's veins. This was just what he needed to get his mind off everything. They unloaded the kayak and started up the rocky trail. "Did you find a place where we can dive from the helicopter?"

"Dani's thinking Nantahala Lake. We've gotta figure out how high, though."

"How far was the one from that video we watched?"

"Seventy-five feet into the Hudson, but he was a high dive world champion."

"So we're going for eighty?"

Wes laughed. "I was thinking eighty-five."

"Good, it'll keep me from getting soft now that training's over." He'd been too exhausted during the eight weeks of BTOC to do much else. Part of him thought he shouldn't do anything that'd pin him down again. But most nights weren't nearly this exciting.

Most days weren't as much fun as yesterday had been, either. He thought of Faith, covered in paint, leaning in to tell him he was going gray.

Connor readjusted the kayak, his arms starting to burn from holding it up. First he'd throw himself into this adventure. Then he'd try to figure out how far he was willing to push his boundaries with Faith Fitzpatrick.

. . .

Faith told herself she wasn't purposely avoiding Connor, but the problem with lying to yourself was that you knew you were full of crap. She'd occasionally hear his low voice when he picked up Kaleb, so she'd stay in her room and wait until she was sure he was gone to get up and go for her run. Her time was improving—she could make it two miles without having to walk now. By the end of next week, she hoped to push it to three.

In the early afternoons, she'd go work at the park. Anna and Ella came one day, and one of Anna's friends had helped Faith do the second coat on the gazebo. Mrs. Lowery had come by and told them that it'd do, which was pretty much the highest form of praise she gave.

With her "volunteer" work done, she'd spent a few days scouting apartments in Charlotte. She'd found several nice places, a couple close to the college. Too bad they all wanted to see her pay stubs, which were impossible to produce, since her internship didn't start until the beginning of next semester and was unpaid anyway. A couple of landlords said they'd take two months' rent in advance, but with her money still tied up in the stupid condo she didn't even live in anymore, she didn't have that yet, either.

So for now, it looked like she'd be staying with Kaleb

longer than she originally planned. She'd just finished filling out a couple of student loan applications to help her eventually get an apartment when she heard Kaleb's and Connor's deep voices in the living room, yelling at the TV screen, like that'd make a difference in whatever sporting event they were watching.

Guess I knew I couldn't avoid a run-in with him forever. Faith undid her bun, shook out her hair, and did a quick makeup check—because she might go out, not to impress Connor. Yeah. She'd *totally* go out.

When she entered the living room, Kaleb was the only one on the couch. A twinge of disappointment went through her, as stupid as that was. She almost asked him about Connor, but then he'd want to know why she was asking, and she didn't even know why.

It's better this way. The more space she gave him, the more likely he was to move on to a new girl. Then she'd know she'd made the right choice and could stop thinking about his sexy laugh and handsome face.

She headed to the kitchen to grab a drink and ran into a solid brick wall of muscle. Connor's hands gripped the sides of her waist as he grinned down at her. "I was wondering if you were going to hide in your room all night."

"I wasn't hiding."

"You've been avoiding me for days."

"No, I've been busy. Not everything's about you, believe it or not." Her blood pumped faster and hotter and her chest filled up with the breaths that had suddenly forgotten how to move in and out of her lungs. Now she was remembering why it was best to keep herself from running into him. He was so frustratingly egotistical.

"Busy doing what?" His translucent gray eyes bored into her and she found it hard to focus with his strong fingers still gripping her waist, the heat from them seeping into her skin.

One of his dark eyebrows rose higher than the other. "I'm making conversation here. Asking about what's going on with you. I hear that's what friends do."

Faith expelled a shallow breath. "Still trying to find an apartment. I'd like one next to the college, but no one wants to rent to me unless I drop massive amounts of cash first. So it's not going as smoothly as I hoped it would."

"I can help. Just tell me which apartment complex and I'll make some calls for you."

She lowered her eyebrows. "Are you serious?"

"As a heart attack. I'm pretty good at talking people into things." One corner of his mouth turned up and her heart rate hitched up right along with it.

"That's okay. I got it." She pushed past him, needing space so she could stop thinking about how nice his hands felt on her body, and opened the fridge. She pulled out a SoBe water, leaned back against the counter, and took a large gulp. "You look pretty paint-free."

"Right back at you."

Faith pulled a section of her bangs forward, sliding her fingernails down it. "I've still got a little here and there. Luckily it blends in okay."

"I was going to help you with the other coat, but Mrs. Lowery told me it was all taken care of. She gave me another assignment, though."

"Let me guess—it was so nice of you to volunteer for it."

Connor laughed. "You got it. You're now looking at the guy in charge of manning the Cornelius Food Drive. She wants to get it started at the festival and have the station be the drop-off quarters, so that the town's got everything it needs by Thanksgiving."

"I suppose despite her slave-driver tendencies, Mrs. Lowery means well."

For a moment they just stared at each other, like they

were trying to see who'd make the next comment or move.

Then Anna came into the room, Ella trailing behind her and whining for something Faith couldn't make out. "Sorry," Anna said. "I thought Kaleb was in here, and I was going to see if he'd keep Ella entertained for a while. She's being so dramatic tonight."

Ella frowned, sticking her lip out so far it nearly touched her chin. "I not dramatic." All day she'd been crying over little things, from asking to watch *Sleeping Beauty* again the second it'd ended, to not wanting to eat her veggies and tossing them to prove her point, to not getting the *right* princess cup.

Connor slung his arm over Faith's shoulders. "Faith and I will take her out for ice cream. That oughta cheer her up."

Within seconds, Ella's face transformed to a huge smile. "Ice cream!"

"If that's okay," Connor said, way too late, because a "no" wouldn't go over very well. And wait a second, he was volunteering her for this trip? This wasn't the kind of going out she'd meant. In fact, this was the kind of going out that got her in deeper. The way her body reacted to Connor made it clear that being alone with him, at least until she found another guy to crush on, was a bad idea.

Kaleb came in. "I heard my name. What do you need?"

Faith was about to suggest Kaleb and Connor go, when Anna winced and threw a hand to her stomach.

Kaleb put his palm on her shoulder and leaned down to her eye level. "Hon? You okay?"

She waved a hand through the air. "Fine. Just overdid it today, I think. Been on my feet too much."

"You get her taken care of," Connor said to Kaleb. "Faith and I are taking Ella to get a treat." He glanced at Anna, and she nodded.

"The car seat's in the van," Anna said, "so it'll probably be easiest to take that. Keys are in my purse. I'll grab them and then you can—Ouch."

"I got it," Faith said. "Go relax." She eyed her brother, not liking the worry creasing his features. Was this normal? Kaleb mouthed "thanks" and helped Anna out of the room. Faith scooped up Ella, dug the keys out of Anna's bag, and headed to the garage with Connor.

Once Ella was strapped in and the van door was closed, Faith dropped the keys in Connor's open palm. "She's gonna be okay, right?"

Connor wrapped his fingers around her hand, the keys smashed between them, and nodded. "She'll be fine. It's just regular pregnancy stuff."

"And you know this how?"

"I've got two sisters," he said, and her tensed muscles finally relaxed. He turned and opened the van door. Then he undid his act of chivalry by checking out her butt and making an appreciative noise as she climbed in. When she glanced back at him, he shrugged as if he couldn't help it. How could he be so reassuring one second and such a one-track-mind guy the next?

And why did she find the combination so freaking hot?

He winked at her as he fired up the van and all she could do was shake her head. She bit back a smile at how out of place he looked behind the wheel of a minivan. There he was, his white T-shirt showing off his muscles, driving a giant vehicle that screamed *your life of being cool is beyond over.* And he still had a giant grin on his face. He had a couple-days' growth lining his jaw, the dark stubble only emphasizing the strong line of it.

He caught her staring and waggled his eyebrows. Heat flooded her cheeks, and she worked to recover. "The minivan suits you. I think you should get one."

"Sweetheart, I already have to beat the ladies off me with a stick. If I get one of these bad boys, I might cause a riot."

"Do you ever stop?"

"I can go all. Night. Long."

Faith's mouth dropped open. She glanced back at Ella, who was watching the town go by out her window and then reached over and smacked Connor's arm. "Behave. We've got a kid in the car, you know."

"I want to ask you something, actually. And since I've got you trapped, it seems like as good a time as any..." Connor slowed for a stoplight and glanced at her. "Go out with me Saturday."

"Connor, I—"

"Don't answer now. In fact, don't answer until you're gonna say yes." He pulled up in front of the shop and glanced back at Ella. "Who's ready for ice cream?"

"Me!" Ella tugged on the straps of her car seat, trying to get free. Connor was out of the van and helping her before Faith could even come up with a response to his first question—the hard question. The second one was so much easier. Who wasn't ready for ice cream?

When they got into the shop, Connor leaned Ella over the display so she could see all the flavors. Her eyes widened as they took in the ice cream. Keeping one arm tightly around Ella's waist, Connor scooted next to Faith and put his hand on her back. "So what's your poison?"

Men who look like you.

"Pink!" Ella yelled, squirming to face Connor. "I want pink!"

"Shocker," Faith joked, poking her niece's stomach so that she giggled. "Let me guess, sprinkles, too?"

Ella bobbed her head enthusiastically.

Within a few minutes, they each had dishes filled with ice cream, all of them with rainbow sprinkles. Not that she'd admit it out loud, but Faith couldn't get over how easily Connor handled Ella, not even flinching when she put her sticky hand over his.

Faith licked chocolate sauce off the back of her spoon. "So how many nieces and nephews do you have?"

"Two nephews. Three nieces—two of them are twins."

Faith's eyebrows shot up. That was a *lot* of kids.

"That's what happens when you've got two older sisters who want big families. Then there's me, and my little brother, who just started college at North Carolina State. When everyone gets together, it's a madhouse."

"I bet." Faith scooped up another bite of ice cream with her spoon. "That must've been fun, growing up with so many siblings." Kaleb had taken care of her, but she'd always wanted a sister.

Connor glanced out the front window. "It's fun now."

Now? She was about to ask him why, but then he smiled and said, "Of course it's that many more people telling you what you should do with your life."

"And what do they think you should be doing? Something less dangerous? Because I'd have to agree."

"No, they're very supportive of my career."

She frowned, a pang going through her chest. She was supportive. Ish.

"I wasn't saying…" Connor placed his hand on her knee. "You went through something awful—something no one should ever have to deal with. I know it's different for you."

The dull ache that never quite went away throbbed at the mention of Dad's death. In some ways it was nice that Connor already knew what happened to Dad, because she didn't have to explain. But in other ways, it felt like he already knew too much. That he could peer inside her at the part she didn't usually let other people see.

"But I want you to know that Kaleb and I know what we're doing," Connor said, his voice reassuring, the pressure of his hand on her knee increasing. "I've got his back, no matter what happens. Okay?"

Faith glanced at Ella, who was scooping up her mostly melted ice cream, happy as could be, then returned her gaze to Connor. One minute he was over-the-top flirting, and then he was staring at her in a way that made her feel like she could spill all her secrets and he'd take care of them. She was tiptoeing a line, and one wrong slip could send her tumbling into his arms.

They were really nice arms, too.

But she couldn't go there. She swallowed and sat back. "It's nice to know. But I'm still going to worry. I can't help it."

"I get it." A grin spread across his face. "Just like I can't help flirting with you because you're so hot."

And there went the sensitive guy. Still, the wicked glint in his eye was making her heart flutter in a way it had no business doing.

. . .

Connor had gone back and forth about asking Faith out, not sure if he dared cross that line or not. But when he saw her tonight in the kitchen… All he knew for sure was that over the past several days, he'd missed seeing her. She was sexy, sure—he couldn't help notice the way her shirt stretched across her breasts and the hint of lace he could see through the pale pink fabric.

Faith cleared her throat, drawing his eyes back to her face, and he gave her a sheepish grin. She'd been staring at him earlier, so he figured they were about even. But it only reemphasized the other reasons he was attracted to her. He had to work to keep up with her. He was never sure where their conversations would go, but the more she talked, the more he wanted to know. He liked how hard she fought to hide her smile when he shamelessly flirted with her, and he liked even more when she lost the battle. That smile stirred a longing deep in his gut that made him crave more.

"All done!" Ella said, tossing her bowl and spoon onto the table. She was covered in chocolate and melted pink ice cream, with a couple of rainbow sprinkles stuck to her cheek. She was a dang cute kid, with as much energy as two of his nieces or nephews combined.

Faith grabbed a wad of napkins and wiped at Ella's face. The kid reared back, ducking away from the napkin. "Just hold still, Ella," Faith said. Pieces of paper clung to the ice cream on her cheeks where Faith had managed to make contact. "I should've brought some of those wipey thingies Anna always has in the diaper bag. These dry napkins aren't doing much against the stickiness."

Ella stood in the highchair, the legs rocking.

Faith shot up at the same time he did. He steadied the chair as Faith pulled Ella out. The two-year-old repaid her by hugging her tightly and wiping her face across Faith's light shirt. "Awesome," she mumbled. "Whose idea was ice cream anyway?" She flashed Connor a look, but there was teasing behind it and it sent a burst of warmth through his chest.

Faith took Ella to the bathroom to clean her up while Connor cleared their table of trash. When she came back, Ella's face was scrubbed clean and Faith's shirt was damp in the spot where she'd had ice cream a moment ago. It made it even more see-through, but he restrained himself from staring.

As they walked outside, he put his hand on Faith's back. She glanced at him but didn't say anything, so he kept it there. "We should go to the park," he said. "Let Ella burn off the sugar high."

Faith lifted her eyes to the dimming sky. "It's getting dark."

"Exactly. We can take her home nice and tired. Trust me,

Kaleb and Anna will thank us."

He put gentle pressure on her back, guiding her toward the crosswalk that'd take them to the park with the playground instead of the van.

She let out a sigh and then gave in to his touch. His heart thudded and he was pretty sure his smile had morphed to a goofy grin, but he didn't care. When they got to the park, Ella wiggled down and tore off toward the plastic jungle gym.

The park was set up with a fence around the smaller playground, perfect for little tykes like Ella and his nieces and nephews. Only one way out, and it was next to the two benches flanking the opening. Genius planning, actually, he'd learned, after one of his nephews made a break for it and he'd barely caught him in time.

Connor took Faith's hand and pulled her onto the nearby bench. She tugged free of his grasp and crossed her arms like they were in some kind of showdown. If they were, he was definitely going to win.

"Shouldn't you be out at the bars right now, picking up gullible, ditzy women?" she asked.

Connor clicked his tongue. "Blondie, Blondie, Blondie. How little you know me." He draped his arm over the bench and wound his fingers through her hair. "Once I set my sights on something…" His eyes moved to her lips. He caught a whiff of her perfume, an exotic yet light scent that made him want to lean closer and take a deep inhale.

"Connor," she said in a warning tone. "You remember we're just friends and can *only* be friends, right?"

"Of course," he said, leaving his hand in the silky strands. "I was hoping *you* remembered. I didn't want to remind you, though, because it'd be so awkward."

She laughed, shaking her head, like she always seemed to when he said anything. "You're too much."

"Or am I just the right amount?"

"Definitely too much."

He let his leg rest against hers, taking deep breaths to control his response to being so close to her—they were at a park, after all. Ella came down the slide with a screech, then immediately tore up the plastic steps again.

Faith glanced at him, the overhead lights glowing in her eyes. "You take on everything headfirst, don't you? Don't think, just act and let the cards fall wherever, no thought to what happens after."

"Is there any other way?" he asked, though she'd pegged him wrong. Sure, on several things he dove right in and figured he'd deal with whatever consequences arose. But when it came to other aspects of his life, like relationships and tying himself to other people, or going into a hostile situation, or even working on a case, he thought things through more than most. "There are things you can control. But then there are times you have to learn to let go and see what happens.

"You know what we should do," he said, and before she could answer or try to change the subject, he quickly charged on. "My friend, Wes, and his fiancée, Dani, have an adventure-tour business. You fly in a helicopter to one of the national parks to hike, cliff dive, or swim in a lake most people don't even know exists—it's such a rush. All your worries, everything—it just disappears for a while."

Two creases formed between her eyebrows. "I'm pretty sure cliff diving into a lake with slimy creatures would give me more worries, not less."

"I should've known you'd be too scared."

She spun to face him. "I am *not* scared."

That obviously hit a sore spot, and he figured he could work with that. "Prove it."

"I don't have to prove anything to you." She twisted to face the playground and went back to her crossed-arm position. "You drive me crazy."

"Right back at you. Just imagine how that chemistry would transfer to the bedr—"

She slapped a hand over his mouth. "Don't finish that."

He grinned under her hand. Getting her all fired up was so damn fun. Possibly contrary to getting her to agree to go out with him, but too addicting to totally give up. He was trying not to think about what her brother would say if he actually talked her into it. He just wanted to focus on being here with her now.

He jerked his chin toward the swings. "Care to see who can go higher?" It was a cheesy move he swore he'd never make, but there was something about this girl that made him want to let go.

Faith didn't answer, but he could see she was thinking about it, so he took her hand and tugged her toward the swings. They waved at Ella as they passed and he sat in one of the seats—man, they really pinched the butt. His legs were dragging, too. This might end up being humiliating instead of winning him points.

Faith sat on the other swing, and soon they were soaring through the air, his feet occasionally dragging the bottom. The higher she went, the more the streetlamp lit up her face, and the bigger her smile got. Connor kept glancing over at Ella's blond head bobbing around, keeping an eye on her as well.

If any of the guys from the department saw this, they'd give him so much hell. But then Faith smiled and kicked his swing, sending him off course, so he didn't really care.

Connor's phone chirped and he dug it out, hanging tight to one side of the swing. A text from Kaleb, checking in. He sent a message that they'd head back in a few minutes and asked about Anna. Got a response that she was fine.

By the time he was done, he was no longer swinging. Faith jumped off her swing and headed over to Ella, who was at the top of the twisty slide. Connor couldn't hear what they were saying, just the low murmur of voices.

He walked up to Faith and put his hand on the small of her back—he'd decided it belonged there. "Ready to go?" he asked.

"Nooo!" Ella shrieked, and ran in the other direction, across the bridge and toward the other slide.

"I'll get her," Connor said. Without a second thought, he leaned in and kissed Faith's cheek.

Her green eyes peered up at him, and he could tell she was about to say that they needed to stay just friends again.

"My bad. I meant, I'll go get her, buddy ol' pal." He gently punched Faith's shoulder and then headed after Ella. As soon as he'd wrestled the wiggly little girl onto his shoulders, he caught back up to Faith. In the two minutes it'd taken to get Ella, Faith had thrown up her walls again. When he neared her, she strode ahead of him.

Somehow he had to show her there was more to him than met the eye. *Like a Transformer,* he thought with a smile. Eventually, he'd get her to go out with him. Then he'd win her over. Whether it was their first date or their twentieth.

That thought brought him up short. He wasn't sure where it'd come from. Twenty dates with *one* girl?

Then he looked at the girl.

For the first time in a long time, he thought that maybe he could get down with that.

Chapter Seven

Faith was going to do it today. She really was this time. She'd survived her first couple weeks of being in Cornelius, seeing all the familiar sights and Daddy's picture in the Rusty Anchor. So today she'd face down the last of her demons. Show that she could employ the stress coping mechanisms she'd learned in college to get through something she'd avoided since she was sixteen years old. That way, when she counseled other people to use them, she could declare that they worked without feeling like a hypocrite. She climbed into her car, telling herself that she was in a tiny town and knew the police station was filled with good guys, including her brother—and, okay, Connor.

Still, her hands shook as she gripped the wheel. She'd always gone out of her way, often taking the longer route, to avoid the area of town where Daddy had been shot. He'd been off duty, fueling up the car at the gas station, when he'd heard gunfire. He'd grabbed his gun, charged into the store, and took out the man firing on innocent people. But he hadn't realized the man's accomplice was in the back of the store. Even after Daddy had been shot, he'd managed to take out the threat, saving everyone else. They'd called him a hero—and he was.

But he was also her dad, and now he was gone.

Faith exhaled a long breath and pointed the AC at her face. After that day, she'd avoided convenience stores for months. Kaleb would fill up her gas tank before she had to ask—once he'd forgotten, though, and she'd run out of gas in the middle of town and had to call him to pick her up. That was about the time Dr. Schaeffer convinced Mom to see a therapist to help her cope, and recommended Faith and Kaleb see one, too.

By the end of her senior year, Faith could visit the gas station on the far end of town, though she'd still dreaded every time she had to fill up. When she'd packed for college, Kaleb had asked if she'd be okay fueling her car on her way to Atlanta. She'd said of course, even though she was secretly afraid she wouldn't be.

It'd been a long time since she'd feared a gas station. But she wanted to prove she wasn't scared anymore. Those criminals didn't determine where she got gas or bought a pack of gum. It was just a store, and her Jetta was low on fuel. The other place was opposite the way she needed to go.

Now I'm building it up too much. Giving it too much power.

Let's see… New perspective. Once I prove it's okay for me to go to this part of town, I can start shopping at Leila's Boutique. She has the cutest necklaces around, and my other one from there got lost in one of my moves.

Connor had mentioned going on an adventure tour. She wanted to be the kind of girl who did something like that, instead of overanalyzing all the ways she could get hurt. She'd always been like that, even before she lost Daddy, but it got even worse after. She'd even moved a few times because she felt like her neighbors might be criminals or that the apartment complex wasn't safe enough. Jeff had accused her of being too scared of everything, which was why it irritated her so much for Connor to do the same.

Funny enough—in the way that wasn't actually funny—guys were the part of her life she'd never analyzed enough. She got all wrapped up in one, in the kissing and butterflies, forgetting all the ways that her heart could get hurt, which was worse than a broken leg or arm in a lot of ways. That was what she'd realized when she'd been hammering out a legal agreement with Jeff, unable to deal with trying to find an internship while she was working through having her trust shattered and her heart broken. But the many ways that guy screwed up her life was a hurdle for another time. First things first: refueling her car.

It's just a tank of gas. Maybe I'll go in and buy a pack of gum before I head to meet Brynn and Paul at the restaurant. Their schedules had made it impossible to set up a day for fishing yet, but it was Paul's birthday, so they were getting together at Cappano's, and it was nice to have plans. It also got her out of the house. She didn't want to give Connor the impression she was always sitting around, waiting for him to show up.

She shouldn't want to go out with him, but after their ice-cream-and-park hangout with Ella the other day… There was something comforting about him, even though he also scared the hell out of her. But if she managed to get through this trip to the gas station, maybe she could do one of those tours—like the swimming-in-an-isolated-mountain-lake one.

And if she imagined Connor with her—shirtless, of course—that was simply because it helped her face her demons. Keeping the image in mind, she slowed so she could turn into the gas station. Empowerment filled her. She could do this.

A guy wearing a jacket, hood on, got out of his car. There wasn't enough light to see him well. There weren't enough lights at all.

Faith slammed on the brakes. The car behind her laid on the horn. She glanced in the rearview mirror and then straightened her wheel and continued down the road. The needle on the gas gauge was nearing the danger zone, and the low-fuel warning flickered on as if to spite her.

Setbacks were common. No need to worry. She'd simply fill up on the way back.

When it was darker.

And later.

Oh, hell. She might have to call Kaleb to pick her up again.

When the waitress at Cappano's pointed Faith to the table where her party was waiting, there were way more people than she'd expected.

Brynn came over and hugged her. "Glad you could come." She started going down the line, introducing people. Names kind of went in one ear and out the other, until she got to the couple at the end. "This is Wes and his fiancée, Dani."

Faith was sure Connor had mentioned both those names. "You wouldn't happen to run an adventure-tour business, would you?"

Wes set down the glass he'd been drinking from. "I do, actually. Hopefully you've heard good things?"

"Yeah, all good." Since everyone was staring at her now, she felt the need to explain. "I know Connor Maguire. He's…" She didn't know if she should say friend of her brother, or her friend, or—

"Here he comes right now," Wes said, raising a hand to

wave behind her.

Faith turned, and sure enough, there he was. His dark hair was messy and he wore a black shirt with the top couple of buttons undone and the sleeves pushed up to show off his forearms. Nice but slightly casual. Perfectly Connor.

His dark eyebrows shot up as he neared her, and a cocky smile slowly took over his surprised expression. "Blondie." He leaned in close, his warm breath hitting her neck. "If you would just call, you wouldn't have to follow me around. I'd give you a ride and everything."

"I was here first," she whispered, working to keep her voice steady, because she knew he'd notice, "so that makes no sense."

"Whatever you say." Connor put his hand on her back, the same way he had the other day, and all her blood seemed to rush to that spot. He nodded at the people seated at the table. "Hey, guys." His gaze moved to Paul. "Happy birthday, man."

Wes glanced from Faith to Connor and his eyebrow twitched up. Connor nodded, and she wondered what that was all about. There was definitely something unspoken going on, but when she looked at Connor to get a read on him, he just pulled out one of the two empty chairs at the table and gestured for her to sit.

Faith glanced at Brynn as she settled into the chair. "How do you know Connor?"

"Wes and Dani were going to set us up, actually." Brynn glanced at Sawyer, who was seated on her other side, and smiled. "But then Sawyer and I got together," she said, and he lifted their entwined hands and kissed the back of hers. "And Paul met him through Wes. They all go fishing and do those tours in the helicopter."

Of course they did. All part of the small-town curse and charm. Here she thought she'd get a break from Mister Serve and Render Speechless tonight, and instead he was draping his arm over her chair, his familiar cologne invading her senses, making her forget that she was solely on the lookout for humble guys now.

Paul explained to his fiancée, Carly, about how his family used to spend time fishing and barbecuing with Faith's family. Faith tensed, waiting for her or someone else to ask why they stopped, but the waiter came, and she breathed a sigh of relief.

After that, it was a blur of ordering and multiple conversations. Everyone was coupled but her and Connor, which made her a little glad she wasn't the only single person, even if Connor was the other. Halfway through the meal, Connor brushed his fingertips over the back of the hand she had under the table. She glanced at him and one corner of his mouth turned up. Her pulse sped up as he slowly covered her hand and laced his fingers with hers.

He was quickly becoming inescapable.

But with her hand in his, she wasn't so sure she wanted to escape him anymore. His big, annoying presence always managed to calm her nerves as much as fluster them. And she couldn't deny she wondered what it'd be like to kiss him. To do more... Her body heated and her heartbeats tripped over each other.

This is exactly why I need to avoid him. My common sense flies right out the window, and I start thinking I don't need it anyway. She tugged free of his hold, under the guise of getting her drink.

Only Connor simply wrapped his large hand around her thigh and a flurry of butterflies swarmed her stomach. He glanced at Wes. "I'm trying to convince Faith to go on one of your tours with me."

"They sound lovely and all," Faith said, "but I think I'm more of a sit-in-a-boat or take-a-swim-in-Lake-Norman girl.

Not get into a helicopter to go cliff diving or take a hike that makes me wanna cry."

Wes put his arm around Dani. "I used to have a hard time getting her up in the air, but she's gotten over it. Probably because I'm the best pilot this side of the Mississippi."

Dani dramatically rolled her eyes so Wes would catch it, and Faith immediately liked her. Wes pulled his fiancée close and whispered something in her ear that made her blush, then sat back with a smug grin on his face. What was it with guys here? Cockiness must run in the water. She supposed she wouldn't want to get in the air with a pilot who wasn't confident. Still, she wouldn't want to go without Connor by her side, and the whole problem with that was she shouldn't *want* Connor by her side.

"You could come on one of the mild tours," Dani said. "There's a place with a waterfall that feeds into a lake, and there's this amazing cave behind it where the water trickles down and the sunlight filters in." She smiled, a dreamlike look on her face. "It's beautiful."

"It's a date," Connor said.

"Not so fast," Faith started. But then everyone was looking at her. Maybe she should simply dive in. Would an adventure really be so bad?

"I'll be there every step of the way," Connor said, squeezing her thigh and sending a spark of electricity through her core. Damn him and his low voice and strong fingers.

Faith took a deep breath, trying to decide how hard she was going to fight spending time with Connor when all she wanted to do was give in. After all, finding new hobbies was a healthy coping mechanism. And if she could accomplish an adventure tour and face that mild fear in a controlled environment, she'd learn more skills to face her stronger fear of the gas station. It'd be research, really. Research with a very tempting guy.

"Okay, one mild adventure." Faith locked eyes with Connor. "But if anything happens to me, my ghost is totally going to come back to haunt you."

As usual, he took her threat as some kind of compliment, a giant grin on his face.

After making a few more minutes of small talk, Connor leaned over, his lips near her ear, and a tingle of anticipation traveled down her spine. "You wanna get out of here?"

She peered into his eyes, thinking yes, yes she did, and at the same time, how very bad an idea that was, considering his nearness caused her thoughts to go fuzzy. Somehow her brain didn't get the message about that last part, though, and she found herself nodding.

• • •

Connor couldn't believe his luck. Faith had ended up at the party, had agreed to an adventure tour, and was leaving with him. He barely resisted spiking the napkin onto the table and breaking into a celebratory touchdown-type dance.

They said their last good-byes and made their way out of the restaurant. Connor kept hold of her hand—he was afraid otherwise she might realize she willingly agreed to spend time with him and take off running.

While he'd love nothing more than to take her back to his place, he knew he had to tread carefully. So he led her between the buildings and down to the shore of the lake, sticking to the longer grass. The water lapped the shore, the constant sound mixing in with the chirp of crickets.

"So you used to go fishing with the McAdamses?"

Faith nodded. "All the time. Paul Senior and my dad were friends." She hesitated, and he thought of how she'd flinched at the restaurant, as if she were waiting for the conversation to go downhill. But then a small smile touched her lips. "We'd load up the tackle boxes and coolers and head to the middle of the lake. We'd fish and swim—our dads always muttered about our splashing scaring away the fish. I used to complain that it was all we did every weekend, but now, those are some of my best memories. I caught a couple of huge fish, too. Gave the boys a run for their money."

"I remember the day I almost caught a record-breaking fish," Connor said.

Faith glanced up at him, the moonlight dancing in her eyes. Damn, she was pretty. So pretty, he almost forgot he was in the middle of a story.

"Every time I yanked, I felt it tugging against me, trying to drag the other way. My arms ached, but I didn't want to let it go. I was about eight or nine, and I could already see headlines in the local paper, about the boy who caught the giant fish. Total hero stuff, you know." He tightened his grip on her hand, loving how tiny hers felt in his. "I finally pull it in, see the water parting for the giant beast... And it was a bucket."

The dimple in Faith's cheek came out full force. "A bucket?"

"I was so disappointed. I fished the rest of the day, determined to make up for it. And of course all I caught were a couple tiny black crappies that I swore were laughing at me every time I pulled them out of the water." That was back when he'd tried so hard to impress Dad because he wanted to be like him. Back before he knew what was going on or why Mama spent so much time alone in her room.

He took a breath of fresh air and blew out the bad memories with his exhale. Right now he wanted to think about nothing but being with Faith. His place was close now, only a couple houses away, and he couldn't decide if he should bring it up or not. He'd walked to the restaurant, and he was sure her car was back there.

"There was a picture in my daddy's study of me with the

first fish I caught, and it was almost as big as I was. Seeing how proud he was…" Faith's voice cracked and it shot him right through the heart. "That was when I declared I was going to grow up to be a fisherwoman. He told me if I figured out how to make a living at it that I should go for it. Of course a couple of months later, I decided I'd rather be a mermaid instead—cheaper living and all, since the lake would be my house."

Connor grinned at her. "You'd make a great mermaid."

She laughed. "A seashell bra, though? No way that's comfortable."

Now his mind was diving into the gutter again. "Well, there are the topless kind of mermaids, too. Always a good option."

Faith shoved him—surprisingly hard, too, for as little as she was. He wrapped his arm around her waist, curling her to him. He could feel her curves against him, hear the sharp intake of breath.

Normally, he wouldn't think twice about kissing her. He'd simply do it. But with her insisting they be just friends, he felt like every move he made could push her away.

Almost on cue, she tensed.

So he took a step back and kicked off his shoes.

Her eyebrows drew together. "What are you doing?"

"Going for a swim."

She glanced at the still water and then back at him. "You've got to be kidding."

"You're going in, too, so I suggest removing any clothing you don't want to get wet."

"I don't want to get any of it wet."

"Naked, then. Score for me." Connor shot her a smile, unbuttoned his shirt, and tossed it to the ground, the air warm and sticky against his skin. Faith pressed her lips together, trying to look unimpressed, but he caught the way her eyebrows twitched higher. "You've got about one minute, and then I'm throwing you over my shoulder, and we're jumping off the pier. If I were you, I'd at least lose the shoes."

She took another step back and a predatory urge ran through him. Throwing her over his shoulder was going to be fun. "Then I'll have to walk back to my car soaking wet."

"My house is right there." He pointed to the home up the beach, where the back porch light was burning. "You can dry off there, and then I'll drive you back to your car."

Connor unbuttoned his pants and dropped them, leaving on only his black boxer briefs. "Thirty seconds."

"I knew coming with you was a bad idea," Faith said, then peeled off her shirt. She had on a purple-and-white-polka-dot bra, and even though he knew he shouldn't just stare, he couldn't help it. She shimmied out of her shorts, revealing matching panties.

"Go on and take a good look, because this is the last time you'll ever see me in my underwear. In fact, I'm never hanging out with you again."

"Worth it," he said. Then he strode toward her, desire heating him even more when she let out a squeal. He scooped her into his arms, ran down the pier, and jumped into the lake.

Cool water enveloped them. Although it was warmer than when he swam in the early morning, it was still enough to shock all his senses awake. He kicked up to the surface. Faith came up seconds later, taking a deep breath and blinking water from her eyelashes.

She swiped her hand across the top of the water, sending a stream into his face. "I hate you," she said, but there wasn't any malice behind it.

He wiped the water from his face and laughed. Then he tried to splash her back, but she dodged and sent another splash of water at him, catching him right in the eyes. He blindly lunged for her, planning on dunking her, but she was faster than he expected.

She swam farther from the shore, creating ripples across the surface of the lake, and he followed her. After a couple of strokes, he could've overtaken her, but he hung back, enjoying the nice view. The glow of the moon lit up her profile as she stopped and peered at the sky. His gaze locked on her lips and he couldn't stop thinking about kissing her. She turned to face him, her arms gliding back and forth in the water, and he thought of her story earlier.

"For the record, you'd make a good mermaid," he said.

Her lips curved into a heart-stopping smile. "The pay's crap, though, and you have to worry about ending up in a tuna can. It's not all it's cracked up to be."

And there's where she blew other women out of the water. She was a sexy that went beyond looks. Always ready with a retort. He wanted to be real with her, in a way he hadn't attempted to be with anyone. It scared the hell out of him, honestly, but there was an edge of relief to it, too, as though he didn't have to work so hard to be what people expected anymore.

He caught her around the waist and drew her to him, his blood heating at the feel of her skin against his. He didn't try to kiss her. Didn't slide his hand down to her perfect ass like he wanted to.

He simply took in the moment, wishing it never had to end.

Chapter Eight

What are you doing here, Faith? This wasn't part of the plan.
She hugged her arms around herself as Connor unlocked
the back door to his place. The night had felt warm before
their swim, but now her wet underwear was soaking through
her clothes and water was dripping from her hair, onto her
shoulders.

As cold as she was, she was second-guessing her decision
to not walk back to the restaurant for her car and head straight
home. That talk about fishing with Dad had her feeling all
warm and sentimental. Even the swim had reminded her of
summer days in the lake. For the first time in a long time,
she'd managed to focus on good memories without the pain.
So she hadn't pushed away when Connor wrapped his arms
around her. The sight of him shirtless, with his built chest and
holy-mother-of-six-pack abs was enough to make her forget
her name, but he'd also been warm and solid and looking at
her so tenderly, she hadn't wanted the night to end.

But she wasn't sure she was ready for where it was going,
either.

As soon as they stepped inside, Penny came bounding toward the door and nuzzled Connor's knee. He reached down and patted her, greeting her with such affection, that Faith again thought she should turn around and run while she still could. Apparently guys who were nice to kids and dogs were one of her weaknesses. Well, that and the muscles, good looks, and ability to drive her insane while semi-turning her on at the same time.

"Go on into the living room and make yourself comfortable," Connor said. "I'll grab us drinks."

Faith's heart was beating so loudly she worried he could hear it. She needed to keep her head—or recover it. "I bet you say that to all the girls."

He cupped her cheek. "Only the really, really pretty ones." He trailed his fingers down her neck, making her skin break out in goose bumps, and then gave her shoulder a gentle squeeze. He turned toward the kitchen, Penny trailing behind him.

Faith knew he was joking about the pretty ones comment, but still, she couldn't help wondering how many girls had been in her place before. Of course, they probably ripped their clothes off the second they got in the door, and she wasn't going to. Okay, so technically, he'd already gotten her out of her clothes once tonight, but it wasn't happening again. Being with Connor like that was a bad idea. Even if she could see the strong line of his back under his shirt and remembered what it had looked like without all that pesky fabric.

She swallowed past her suddenly dry throat. *You're supposed to be going for nerdy guys now, remember? No more guys who aren't worth the heartache that comes after.*

A tiny voice whispered that maybe a night with Connor would be worth it, but Faith quickly told that voice to shut up. Needing a distraction, she walked around Connor's living room. She studied the one framed picture on the side table by the couch—actually, framed was being generous. It was a plastic stand, propped on the table beside a remote. Connor was in the middle, his arm around a beautiful older woman with his same olive skin tone and dark hair—it had to be his mom. The other guy in the picture was younger but looked a lot like Connor, and then there were two girls, one with the same dark hair and one with light brown hair and paler skin with freckles across the bridge of her nose. Still, they looked enough like Connor she was sure they were the siblings he'd mentioned at the ice-cream shop.

Other than the picture, his decorations were minimal. Just the basics. Super-clean, too, like an inspector might come in and make him drop and give him twenty if things weren't in pristine order.

Then she caught sight of the *Star Wars* collection on top of the entertainment center. She moved closer and tipped onto her toes for a better look. Luke, Leia, Chewie, Han Solo, R2-D2, and C-3PO were arranged on the top shelf. A storm trooper, Darth Vader, and the Death Star were on the other side, though Vader and Luke were right by each other. Close enough to fight. Or hug, depending on if Vader had turned back to the Force or not. A light saber—not really a laser, most likely, though it certainly wasn't the cheap plastic kind—sat behind them.

He's got a nerdy side. A flutter rose up, traveling from her stomach to the place over her heart. *I'm in so much trouble.*

"I started collecting them when I was five," Connor said from behind her and she spun around. "Even got the bed set for my eighth birthday, with sheets and the comforter." One side of his mouth kicked up in a crooked, drool-inducing smile. "You'll have to wait to see if I'm still using them."

Dead-sexy. That was the perfect word for him. Sexy in the way that might actually kill her.

He stepped closer and she could feel her resistance

thinning, like a rubber band that was being stretched too far. "I used to have comic-book figurines, too—still do, but they're all in a box." He pointed his chin toward the *Star Wars* figures. "I couldn't quite stand packing those ones away, though, since they were the start of my decision to keep the world safe."

She stared at him—the playfulness in his eyes, that strong jaw that begged her fingers to brush along it. The contradiction of the way he looked and him talking about a collection he started as a boy was a total turn-on. But how many times had he given this exact same spiel to other women? How many times had he gotten laid because of it?

"I…" she started, not even sure how to finish.

"I noticed you were drinking beer at the Anchor, so I hope I picked right."

She took one of the bottles out of his hand and took a generous swig. Already, her muscles were tightening, readying to spring into action. She shouldn't have come home with him. She should go now.

"Why don't we go ahead and start with *Episode Four*?" he asked, pulling a DVD from his entertainment center.

Without making the conscious decision to sit, her legs buckled, and then her butt was on the couch. It seemed like her body and brain were at war whether or not to stay. But now that she was sitting, it *was* comfortable.

Nerves were bouncing around her stomach, higher and harder, as Connor settled next to her. She was hyperaware of him, so close, yet not quite touching. Every breath made his chest rise and fall—holy hellfire he had a nice chest, and now she was remembering him shirtless again.

Her body gave an involuntary shudder, from him or from being cold, she wasn't quite sure.

"You cold?" he asked.

"A little." She knew it was a mistake—he'd offer to keep

her warm. But to her surprise, he got up, pulled a sweatshirt out of the closet, and handed it to her.

"I must be losing my touch," he said in a teasing tone. "This is usually the less-clothing part of the evening."

"Very funny." Faith tugged on the soft sweatshirt that was several sizes too big and smelled like Connor. "You're never getting this off."

"Speaking of getting off…" A wicked glint entered his eye and she smacked his arm. "What? I was saying that you're sitting on the remote." He lifted the remote from the cushions and turned on the TV, false innocence all over his face.

Penny hopped onto the couch and rested her muzzle in Faith's lap. She patted the dog's head and scratched behind her ears, happy for the distraction.

"I can get her to move if you want," Connor said.

The coarse dog hair tickled her palm. "Don't make her move."

"She rarely snuggles up to anyone but me. Usually I have to make her go outside when I have company because she has jealousy issues."

Another line? The truth? After the severe errors in judgment she'd made with the last guy, she couldn't stop overanalyzing. Couldn't stop thinking that if she let herself slip a little with Connor, she'd fall all the way. She wasn't sure she was breathing anymore—her chest definitely felt too tight.

"Why are you so tense?" Connor asked, bumping his shoulder into hers.

Faith's muscles only tightened further, so much so, they started to ache. "I'm not."

"Whatever you say." He turned on the movie and sat back, his arm against hers, his hand resting lightly on her thigh—the impact was anything but light, though. Yes, the chemistry was definitely there, but she was pretty sure Connor would have chemistry with a toaster.

As the movie started, she relaxed a fraction. *Okay, I can do this. No reason I can't spend a nice evening with a super-hot guy who makes me laugh. I'll just set a few boundaries. I've already made it clear that sex is off the menu. But cuddling…* She leaned back, letting her head rest on Connor's shoulder, the way she'd been tempted to do since he first sat down. He wrapped his arm around her shoulders. Between him and Penny, she was perfectly warm, to the point she was almost getting drowsy.

Yes, cuddling was definitely the way to go. Which led her to thinking about which other lines might be possible to cross.

She glanced up at Connor, watching the lights from the television screen dance across his features. He looked down at her, and his fingers tightened on her arm. Then he was dipping his head, curling her closer.

She tipped up her chin, parting her lips slightly, anticipation zipping across her skin.

Then the doorbell rang and Penny shot off the couch, barking and dancing around in front of the door. With a sigh, Connor paused the movie and got up.

"I saw your light was on, so I thought I'd bring this over and see what you were up to," said a high-pitched feminine voice, a boatload of come-hither in her tone. "I just pulled it out of the oven, and I know you're *always* ravenous."

Nice double entendre. Now there's no having to guess why you're here. Not only did he bring girls here all the time, they showed up for booty calls the second they saw he was home.

"I'm, uh, in the middle of something," Connor said, stepping closer to the door, angling his body to block whoever it was—all Faith caught was tall brunette and an air of desperation. By the time he'd gotten rid of her and come back into the room, a pie plate in his hand, Faith's body had remembered how to work. She stood, the quick change in mood jarring her system.

"My neighbor's always cooking," he said, a sheepish yet still too good-looking smile on his face.

Walking-distance booty calls? Yeah, she was *so* out of here, before she got herself hurt all over again. "I think it's time for me to go." Once she was home, she'd berate herself for being stupid enough to come into Connor's house, even though she knew better.

Connor's smile dropped. "Faith, come on. She's nobody, I swear."

"You call girls you sleep with 'nobody'?"

"I'm not… We're… It's not what you think. It's not like we're in a relationship or anything."

A knot formed in her gut. "I know exactly what it is. That's the problem."

Connor set the pie plate on the side table and then grabbed her hand. "Come on. The movie's barely started, and I was looking forward to watching it."

Faith slid her hand out of his. "This was a mistake. We'll just stick to being friends and…" She looked in his eyes and couldn't believe the disappointment coursing through her veins. "I need to go." She started toward the back door, the way they'd come in.

Connor reached it the same time she did. "Hold on, I'm not going to let you go alone. If you're determined to leave now, I'll walk you back."

She wanted to say she didn't need him and charge into the darkness. While the rational part of her brain knew it was a safe town, she also realized that walking around alone this late at night was on the chancy side. There was brave and then there was being careless.

Connor whistled and Penny came running. "Looks like we're all going for a nice evening stroll." How could he be so calm when she felt like something was breaking inside of her? And how had she let him have this much of an effect on her already? She'd sworn she was being more careful.

At least I stopped it before it went too far.

"I'd drive you," Connor said, "but I had three beers tonight between the restaurant and here. Not feeling the effects so much anymore, but not worth the risk. Penny will be glad for the walk, anyway." He opened the door and they all stepped out.

Kaleb's house wasn't too far from here. A little farther than the restaurant and in the other direction, but she thought it'd be better to walk there than to get her car and run out of gas halfway home—there was no way she was facing the gas station this late at night. "I'm just going to walk to Kaleb's."

"I thought your car was at the restaurant."

"I'd rather get it later. Like you said, we've been drinking."

He narrowed his eyes, looking like he didn't quite believe her—she'd barely had one sip of beer at his place—but he nodded. "Whatever you want."

With every step, Faith grew more indignant. Did he think she'd really wanna sit around and cuddle after seeing another woman practically throw herself at him? Did he even care the night was ending like this?

Then there was the other thing she felt—something she hated to admit, even to herself. She wanted to prove she could win Connor over from a woman like that. She'd won before.

Only to find out, several months down the road, that she'd actually lost.

So, sexy *Star Wars* collector or not, she didn't need to get attached to a guy who'd hook up with other women, whether it was the neighbor or a random girl in a bar. A big ol' no thanks on feeling like crap when that happened.

She kept her eyes glued straight ahead, not looking at the guy or even his adorable dog. Connor Maguire wasn't the man for her, so there was no reason to wonder what it would've been like to at least kiss him once.

. . .

Connor kept glancing at Faith marching along, arms crossed in his way-too-big sweatshirt. Having her curled next to him, her lips so close to his one moment, only to have her so far away the next made him want to slam his fist into something. He threw his head back and exhaled. Damn, Leah had the worst timing. They'd fooled around last summer, but then she told him another guy wanted her to be his girlfriend. Connor had a feeling she'd expected him to fight for her, but he'd simply told her good luck. When the two of them split a few months back, Leah started showing up now and again with food and an hour or two to kill. Then she'd gone out of town to visit family. But apparently she was back, and he couldn't help wishing she'd stayed gone forever.

He glanced at Faith again and tried to tell himself he didn't care. But dammit to hell, he did. The contrast of their walk to his house earlier, her hand in his as they shared memories, only made this quiet walk more torturous. She was so close, but not laughing. Not holding his hand. Not looking like all her cares had ceased for a while.

Lead filled his stomach. He'd caused that. But what could he do? He couldn't change who he was.

Just when the silence was about to make him poke his eyes out, they reached Kaleb's back gate. The lightning bugs glittered around them, the same way they had the night at the gazebo. But now it didn't feel magical. It felt like they were getting laid and he was being punished for ever having been.

Connor reached inside the gate and unlocked it, opening it up for her. As she stepped forward, he kept hold of the top of the gate, his arm in her way. "You can't be pissed at me for my past."

Fire lit her eyes as she looked up at him. "I can be pissed at you for any gosh darn thing I want, Connor Maguire, so don't tell me when I can and can't be angry." She gave the gate a yank, but he kept hold of it. The woman drove him so crazy he couldn't think straight. He couldn't decide whether to tell her to march her self-righteous self on inside or pull her into his arms and kiss the hell out of her.

His gaze moved to her full lips. Even twisted in anger like they were, his vote was kissing.

"Hey, jackass," she said between gritted teeth. "Let. Go."

Penny sat a few feet back, her head tilted, one ear cocked, watching and waiting. He probably did look like a jackass. But Faith needed to see he could be just as stubborn as she was. He didn't know what he was doing anymore. This girl was driving him crazy. Making him think things he swore he never would.

"Sweetheart, there's no reason to be jealous of other women. I haven't even *wanted* to sleep with anyone else since you showed up. And, Blondie, if you knew me better, you'd know that's saying something about how I feel about you."

A laugh bubbled out of her, the kind of laugh that's filled more with pain and doubt than happiness. "Guys like you don't change. We both know it, so let's not kid ourselves."

He didn't like the way she lumped him in with other guys who were obviously jerks—he had good reasons for living his life this way. He stared into her big green eyes and said the most sincere thing he could. "I'm not saying I know how to be an awesome boyfriend. But for you, I'd be willing to try."

Faith flinched, like his words had hurt her. He didn't get it. He was offering all he could here, and she was acting like he'd struck her.

He cupped her chin and leaned his head down so they were eye-level. "Faith."

"Please let me go," she said, her voice raw.

Connor's gut twisted, and while he wanted to do something, anything, to fix her sadness, he couldn't deny her when she asked like that. He reopened the gate, swinging it wide. He and Penny stood on the grass and watched her go through the backyard. He waited until she was safe inside and then turned and made the achingly quiet walk home.

Chapter Nine

Faith hoped a night of sleep would erase last night from her head, but the second she woke up, she remembered the way Connor had stood there and said, *I'm not saying I know how to be an awesome boyfriend. But, for you, I'd be willing to try.*

For a moment the words had hung in the air like sparkly, hope-filled little lightning bugs. But then she'd heard Jeff's voice in her head, his words so similar. *I told you from the beginning I wasn't good at relationships.*

Then came the tumbling images of walking in on him and the girl from his office, in flagrante, each second a painful freeze-frame seared into her brain. It was bad enough he was with someone else, but Faith had thought of Lisa as a friend. After all, they'd had meals together. Faith had set her up with guys so they could double.

And Faith had just stood there staring as they tried to cover themselves with the sheet, a hundred excuses exploding from both of their mouths. Things like "It just happened," "It has nothing to do with you," and the killer—"I told you from the beginning I wasn't good at relationships."

As if it were her fault for asking him to be her boyfriend in the first place. For thinking that buying a place together implied a deeper level of commitment.

When he'd told her he couldn't go listen to her big presentation, she should've known he was staying home for more than work. It wasn't like he'd ever been one of those guys who lived for his job. He blew it off for things like golf or a last-minute trip all the time. As soon as the shock wore off—well, enough to move—she'd sprinted out of the condo and down the stairs, gotten into her car, and driven away. She'd wanted to drive out of town, to somewhere else, anywhere else. But she had a monthly mortgage and credit-card bills for things like a new bed, dining room table, and couch, and she'd refused to let that lying jerk get everything after what he'd already taken from her.

Of course he hadn't just agreed to buy the condo or pay for the furnishings he was still using until she'd dragged in a lawyer.

Faith threw her covers over her head and groaned. Why did it continue to sting, even though he'd been the one to do something wrong? It wasn't so much the guy, but the betrayal of trust. She'd even spilled her guts to a certified therapist and the you-got-cheated-on thorn was still in her side.

I can't get over the fact that my ex was a cheater, and I can't get gas at the station where Daddy died. Talking it out, all those years of therapy and everything I've learned, and I'm still screwed up. I'm a fraud, and my whole career's a fraud.

The loneliness she'd fought for years crept up, wrapping its suffocating tentacles around her. She felt herself falling into that dark place that seemed to want her so badly. It whispered to give up. That she'd never be enough for a guy. That she was alone.

Faith heard the door creak open and then the pitter-patter of little footsteps.

"Auntie Faith," Ella whispered, right next to Faith's covered head. Then the covers slid down and Ella's chubby cheeks came into view.

And just like that, light pierced the darkness, pushing it away.

Faith covered a yawn. "Good morning, pretty princess."

Ella climbed onto the bed, struggling for a moment, before getting herself all the way on. "Can we paint nails? 'Cause look." Ella shoved her fingers so close to Faith's eyes that she saw double. The pink had chipped off at the edges, and apparently Ella was one of those girls who couldn't deal with anything less than flawless nails.

Faith sat up against the headboard. She should go running, since she was still training, but she didn't want to. Surely a day off was in order, especially since she'd done double duty yesterday—a run in the morning and a swim at night. "Just let me take a shower and we'll fix them, okay?"

"Yay, yay, yay!" Ella jumped on the bed and then dived onto Faith, hugging her neck so tightly her airway was in danger of being cut off. But Faith didn't let go. It reminded her that she wasn't alone. No matter what happened, she had family, and she thanked her lucky stars that she didn't live so far away from them anymore.

Now she just needed to figure out a way to avoid her brother's friend and partner. Because Connor, the hero-complex player, with his promises to try, could quickly undo the little bit of healing she'd done. And as of right now, she was back on the No Heroes, No Players Wagon.

With that thought in mind, she took a quick shower. Ella came in as she was coating her eyelashes with mascara and ended up getting full makeup, along with freshly painted nails.

"Wow," Anna said when the two of them walked into the kitchen.

Faith grabbed an apple out of the fruit basket. "Hope it's okay. I can't seem to say no to the girl." She leaned against the counter and crossed one ankle over the other. "So, what's on the agenda today?"

Anna boosted Ella onto the counter and handed her a string cheese. "I'm taking Ella to story time at the library, and then I've got to go dig through the community center for the fall decorations. Now that the gazebo's repaired and looking brand new, all we've got left to do is wrap the fake leaves around it and strategically place the pumpkins and hay bales throughout the park. But we'll do most of that just a few days before. I can't believe we only have two weeks left until the festival." Anna ran a hand through her hair. "I sure hope I'm not forgetting anything."

"I noticed the stands that Kaleb made in the backyard." When she'd come in last night, she'd noticed the white pillars of varying heights next to the studio.

"Yeah, he finished them up yesterday after work. I'm going to put them in the tent so all my pieces can be easily seen when people walk by."

"Well, if you want, I'll tag along and help wherever I can. And then when we're done, can you take me by Cappano's? I left my car there."

"Of course. You sure you're up for all the errands? I'm sure it'll be boring."

Faith shrugged. "I've got nothing else to do." And with any luck, it'd keep her mind busy—sitting around might lead her to think about the very thing she was trying to not think about. Maybe tomorrow she'd even take another trip to Charlotte. Swing by the medical school and remind herself what she was working toward. Between what'd happened in Atlanta and the shuffle, she'd lost sight of her goals, and she wasn't going to do that again. She wanted to finish her internship and become a certified counselor.

All day she focused on that and enjoying being around Anna and Ella, helping out whenever she could. They ate lunch at the diner and scheduled a time to meet up with Mr. Landcaster early next week, since he was supplying the hay bales for the park and running the hay rides for the festival.

By the time Faith made it to her car that afternoon, she felt like the pieces of her new life plan were already coming together—she'd just been focusing on all the wrong things. A hint of fall weather hung in the air, and a few of the leaves on the trees were even starting to change—fall might actually arrive just in time for its celebratory festival. When she turned the key, she noticed her car took a little longer than usual to start. Okay, she was definitely going to have to face THE gas station. Good thing today was the day she was getting her life together again. And once she succeeded, she was rewarding herself with jewelry.

She took a deep breath and pulled onto the road. She drove toward the gas station, slowing a bit when the sign for it came into view. *I can do this.* All she had to do was compartmentalize and restructure. She'd heard it dozens of times.

It was a place to get fuel, and she needed gas to keep her car running, simple as that. There were more safety features in place nowadays. People went there every day and came out just fine.

"Let's do this," she said, even though, technically, she was alone. She pushed on the accelerator, but the car didn't speed up. It was getting slower and slower, more drifting down the hill than speeding up.

"Oh, come on. The light just came on yesterday. Doesn't that mean I get at least ten to fifteen miles?"

The car shuddered in answer. The engine revved as she depressed the gas pedal and then the car died completely. She tried to restart it—at least so she could get it out of the middle of the road—but all she got was a clicking noise. "How embarrassing," she muttered, turning on her hazard lights. Cars started around her, and she picked up her phone. Anna had been heading home to put Ella down for a nap, and Kaleb was at work. Was she really willing to pay a tow truck in order to avoid calling in favors?

She lowered her phone, trying to decide which option was the least awful. When she glanced in the rearview mirror and saw the squad car turn down the road, her heart sank and she prayed with everything in her that it wasn't either of the cops she knew.

$$\bullet \ \bullet \ \bullet$$

Even though there wasn't much going on in town, Connor usually preferred driving the streets to sitting in the office and answering calls or filling out paperwork. Especially since he and Kaleb could shoot the shit all day—it made the hours go by faster. The slow days always made him wonder about moving to a city, where he might make a bigger impact and do more with his SWAT training. But he'd miss it here. He liked his mornings running next to or swimming in the lake, serving in a town where he knew most everyone, and working with his best friend.

He leaned forward, peering out the windshield. There was a white Jetta in the middle of the road, the hazard lights blinking.

"Oh, Faithie," Kaleb mumbled. He pulled the squad car behind the Jetta and flipped on the lights.

Connor tensed. Last night he'd put himself out there— not even realizing he was going to do it until it was out of his mouth—only for Faith to shove it in his face. The rejection took him back to those awful junior high days, too, and he hated it, to say the least. He'd planned on avoiding her for a while.

So *of course* it was her car in the middle of the street. Working in a big city was suddenly looking better by the minute.

Kaleb got out of the car, and Connor decided he might as well, too. His partner would probably wonder what was going on if he didn't.

The door of the Jetta opened and Faith exited the car, her head down.

"I thought you were over this," Kaleb said.

Faith kicked at the ground. "I was. I am. Just not paying attention, is all."

Connor glanced from her to Kaleb, who was pinching the bridge of his nose, then back to her. "What's going on?"

"Nothing." Faith's eyes met his, and he could see the embarrassment in her features. "I ran out of gas. I was on my way there, I swear."

The gas station she must've passed on the way to Capanno's last night was just up ahead. Between Kaleb's reaction and hers, he realized what that gas station meant to Faith, and the pieces of the puzzle started dropping into place. "Put it in neutral and we'll get it off the street."

She nodded and got back inside. Connor and Kaleb pushed the car to the side of the road. Kaleb shook his head. "She used to do this all the time in high school. She swore she was over it. I think I only made it worse when I used to fill her tank for her. She's gotta learn to face it sometime."

Connor could feel the exasperation coming off Kaleb, and he didn't want him to aim it at Faith, not when she'd already looked so humiliated. "You move the squad car," Connor said. "I'll talk to Faith." When Kaleb looked like he might argue, Connor patted his shoulder. "Seriously, I got it." He went around to the passenger side of the Jetta and climbed in, closing the door behind him.

Faith ran her thumbnail along the bottom of her steering wheel. "I'm sure Kaleb told you all about my problem. I know, it's stupid. And I swear I was on my way there. I was going to go in this time."

After last night, Connor decided he was done trying to be a guy he clearly wasn't. Thinking he could try a relationship with Faith was a stupid idea anyway. But now she was sitting there, looking…fragile. Not a word he'd usually use for her.

He twisted in the seat to face her and his knee knocked into the glove compartment—he always felt so cramped in these tiny compact cars. "We can play this a few ways. I call in a favor with a tow truck driver I know and we get you to the station on the other side of town, or you can sit here while I go fill up a plastic tank that'll get you at least enough gas to get there. Or…" He tugged her arm from the steering wheel and wrapped his hand around hers. "You go in, with me."

"I'm not scared of going in," she said, her jaw set, but her eyes didn't tell the same story.

"Right. I'm asking you to go with me for purely selfish reasons, actually. I'd rather have you with me."

She shot him one of her signature you're-so-full-of-crap looks.

"Why do it with yourself when you can do it with someone else?" He aimed a smile her way. "That's always been my policy."

The corners of her mouth quivered, and then she not only smiled, but laughed. The sound ignited a dozen fireworks in his chest. His new goal in life was going to be making her laugh. She glanced toward the gas station and all happiness drained out of her expression. She blew out a long breath and turned her eyes on him. "Okay. I'll go with you."

They both got out of the vehicle. "We're walking," Connor said to Kaleb—he didn't think putting her in the back of the squad car like a criminal would help the situation. Besides, the walk would give her a chance to collect herself, and he could tell she needed that.

Kaleb popped the trunk and tossed Connor the plastic gas can they kept inside. He raised his eyebrows, silently asking Connor if he was sure about this. Connor nodded. He wanted to take Faith's hand, but he was very aware of Kaleb watching them.

For a moment, they walked in silence. Then he said, "Had to watch the movie with myself last night. Even Penny fell asleep." He didn't want to bring up a sore subject, but he wanted her to know that as frustrated as he was after she left, he didn't call Leah.

Faith's eyes darted around the area like she was on patrol. It made him do a cursory glance as well. "I was going to give Kaleb your sweatshirt to give to you, but I figured he'd have too many questions, so you can get it the next time you come by. Or I could drop it off."

"I'd prefer the drop-it-off option." He put his hand on her back, figuring he could at least get away with that—with both Fitzpatricks. Faith's steps slowed as they neared the station, until he felt like he was practically pushing her forward. Her skin paled and he could see her chest rising and falling with quick breaths.

"Faith."

Her eyes stayed glued to the station.

"Look at me."

For once in her life, she actually did something he said. He took her hand. "I'm trained, armed, and you're safe with me."

"My dad was trained and armed," she said, glancing at the ground.

He had a dozen things he could say about that, how her dad was off duty, and therefore, not wearing his vest. He was against two shooters. He was trying to save others' lives before his and didn't wait for backup, which Connor admired the guy for, even though it was a more dangerous option. But he didn't think any of those would help Faith right now. It was probably time to let her in on his connection to her dad, though. Well, part of it at least. "Did you know your dad was the reason I became a cop?"

Her head jerked up.

"Like I said last night, *Star Wars* was the start of my wanting to be a hero. But your dad, he was a real hero in the real world."

"I know he was a hero," she said, and her voice cracked. Tears shimmered in the corners of her eyes. "It's just knowing it was here. At this gas station. I feel stupid for not being able to perform a function as simple as getting gas. Especially since I'm going into a career where I'm supposed to help counsel people to get over their fears. But it doesn't make me less afraid."

Connor cupped her cheek, brushing his thumb across the top of it. "I know, baby. But I've been trained to handle dangerous situations. I have a gun strapped on my belt and a partner a few blocks back. I got you."

He stared into her clear green eyes, the overwhelming urge to protect her growing stronger by the second. "I got you."

• • •

Faith's breath was lodged in her throat, all her words gone to wherever her fear had also disappeared to when Connor touched her. It was the most intimate moment she'd ever had in public, the cars driving on the street and the people around fading away. It was just him and her, and they could take on anything. She didn't want to think about how much she was failing at avoiding Connor right now. The important thing to focus on was getting over her fear of a stupid gas station. Taking on one problem at a time—it was part of her training and everything, so it had to be a solid idea.

She took the gas can from him and grabbed onto his other hand. That way he'd have one hand free to draw his gun if needed. And while she knew that was unlikely, it was also nice to know.

Her knees shook when they walked over to the gas pump, but she gripped the handle of the tank and Connor's hand tighter. He pulled out his wallet and she had to race him to get her card slid first. He grabbed the nozzle before she could, though. He filled up the tank as full as it could go, capped it, and lifted it. "Anything else?"

Faith glanced toward the front doors of the store. She was so close, and everything in her wanted to flee, but she still had one thing to check off her list before she'd consider this trip a total success. "I'm buying a pack of gum."

"Okay."

Her heart hammered as she stepped inside. The contrast of the warm day and icy-cold air conditioning made her skin even clammier. When her footsteps faltered, Connor gripped her hand tighter. His other hand wasn't free anymore, but she wasn't sure she could let go. He glanced around the area and gave her a sharp nod.

She tossed a pack of Big Red gum on the counter, paid for it as fast as humanly possible, and then took Connor's hand and nearly sprinted out of the store. Her muscles shook from the adrenaline, but the farther away they got, the easier it was to breathe. She glanced at the jewelry store, her reward for learning to go near the station. But she decided she'd done enough for today. Especially since she wasn't sure that small container of gas would get her across town, and that meant she'd have to pull up to the pumps and finish filling her car.

Still, she'd gone in...

With Connor's help.

She glanced at him, his large profile lit up by the sun. After everything that'd happened last night, she deserved for him to tell her to deal with her problems herself. Kaleb would've lectured her the entire time. Yet Connor just let her use him to hold herself together, strong where she struggled. A hot flush swirled through her chest. "You're making it really hard to resist you, Connor Maguire."

A slow smile spread across his face and his fingers curled tighter around hers. "That's the idea, babe."

"I'm sorry about last night. I've been hurt before, and I'm trying not to make the same mistakes. But I shouldn't have stormed off like that, and I can't thank you enough for what you just did for me." Another few steps and her brother would be able to see their every move. So before she lost the chance, she tipped onto her toes and kissed his cheek.

• • •

Connor couldn't remember the last time he'd smiled for this long, but he didn't care to stop. They'd gotten Faith's car running and followed her to the gas station, where she filled up. By herself. Even though he'd wanted to go hold her hand, he could see the sense of accomplishment on her face when she waved and got back into her car.

He couldn't stop thinking about that kiss she'd given him. He decided right then and there that cheek kisses were totally underrated.

He sat back in his seat, trying to get comfortable for the second round of patrol. Every time Faith brought up the danger element of his job, he wanted to make a joke about how he was more likely to get a permanently flat butt or paper cuts doing reports than shot at. Luckily he'd had the good sense to hold it back—definitely not the thing to say to a girl whose father had been shot. He'd like to believe things would be different now. He'd felt a shift between them, but he knew better than to think she'd easily admit it, if nothing else because she was the most stubborn woman he'd ever met.

Connor turned toward Kaleb, who hadn't said much since they'd refueled Faith's car. Out of respect for the guy, he couldn't put off the uncomfortable chat they needed to have any longer. "What if I like your sister?" He'd never been one to dance around a subject. Now it was out there, so he could see just how pissed Kaleb got.

Kaleb's knuckles turned white as he tightened his grip on the steering wheel. "You don't."

"I do. She's different."

Kaleb sighed and finally glanced at him. The line of his jaw was tense, and he had the kind of look in his eye that perps got when they decided it'd be a good idea to take on an officer. "She *is* different," he said, his words sharp as ice picks. "She's *my little sister.*"

"I know." A rock formed in Connor's gut. He'd take a bullet for the guy sitting next to him, no second thought. "I'm not talking a one-night stand. I want to take her out. See what happens if I give the relationship thing a chance."

Kaleb rubbed a hand across his forehead. "I think that's worse."

"I could use your help, man. I don't want to screw it up before it even starts."

Kaleb shook his head. Luckily he needed his hands to drive, because the guy looked like he wanted to take a swing at him. "You must be tripping, dude. I'm not going to tell you how to get my sister to fall for you so you can end up being a dick to her when you get sick of her. She's had enough of that."

The words pricked his chest, especially after all the time he'd spent at Kaleb's house with him, Anna, and Ella. "That's really what you think of me?"

Kaleb pressed his mouth into a tight line. "You're like my brother. But I've seen you with women. And I don't want to think about you and her... No. Just no."

"I'm not asking for permission. I'm letting you know that I'm going to ask her out. I guess I'm hoping for a little understanding."

An angry vein popped out in Kaleb's forehead. Great. Now he'd have to spend the rest of the day in a car with his pissed-off best friend. He should've waited until the end of the day to bring it up. Faith had accused him of diving in without thinking before, and he was starting to see her point. Maybe he should think things through better. He'd always gotten himself out of trouble before, though. He'd figure out something. Of course, in this case, Kaleb could try to persuade Faith not to go for him. He wasn't the interfering type, though.

Usually.

Kaleb's eyes hardened, his gaze fixed on the road ahead of them. "Doesn't matter what I think. She'll never go for you. Not long-term, anyway."

Connor liked a challenge, but Kaleb's words, combined with what he knew about Faith, made it seem like more than that. "I'm smart, strong—and good-looking, as I'm sure you noticed as we ride around all day." He hoped the joke would ease some of the tension. "And I'm—"

"A cop," Kaleb said, as if the words were a death sentence. "Say she gets over your player past and you two actually work out, she's not strong enough for this lifestyle. You saw how she was today."

Connor opened his mouth to argue that she was strong. She only needed someone to help her—needed *him*.

"She'd spend every day stressed out and scared you wouldn't come home. She'd end up depressed and a shell of herself, just like my mom. Faith doesn't need that life, and I don't want it for her. Maybe that makes me a hypocrite, considering I'm a cop, too, but I don't care. It's my job to protect her, and she's got a bright future ahead of her. I'm asking you to let her be."

With every sentence, Connor's protest faded more and more. Kaleb hardly talked about his mom. Between what Connor heard through town gossip and the few serious talks he and Kaleb had had over the past few years, Connor knew she'd spiraled into a deep depression after her husband was killed. Kaleb had basically taken over at eighteen, everything from running the house to taking responsibility for Faith. His mom had since moved in with her parents and hardly visited. Faith had stayed away till now, and obviously she was still affected by her father's death.

Connor knew what it was like to have a mother who was a shell of herself. To see someone so broken he didn't know if she'd ever be okay again. He'd never wanted to be responsible for that kind of damage, which was why he'd made a decision a long time ago not to ever let himself get in that deep with another person.

So he got it, he did. Didn't mean he liked it or that it was easy to swallow. It felt like he'd finally gotten his hands around Faith, and now she was slipping through his fingers. Even more surprising was the incredible sense of loss that immediately filled him when he thought about letting go completely.

Chapter Ten

Faith ran along the lake, telling herself to push for two more minutes and then she could walk for two. She couldn't stop thinking about Connor. He'd helped her confront one of her biggest fears, even after she'd pushed him away. Her heart tugged and she could feel the ghost of his hand on hers, holding her steady. She'd texted him that night, saying she was thinking about taking him up on his offer to help train the last two weeks before the 5K.

And then she'd heard nothing back. Not that night, not the next one. She hadn't seen him since the gas station. Well, until this morning, when she'd glanced out the window and seen him running along the lake with Penny. So it wasn't like he'd stopped. Apparently he just didn't want to run with her, and her mind was spinning out of control, wondering what had happened.

What if he decided I have too many issues? What if now that I gave in the tiniest bit, he's bored with the chase? And the worst: *What if he was too busy with his neighbor?*

Faith kicked faster, sprinting until her thighs burned and

her lungs screamed for air. She pushed past the two-minute mark and made it all the way back to the house. When she stumbled into the kitchen, her breaths still choppy, Kaleb was sitting at the table, sipping a cup of coffee.

"You're up early," he said.

"I thought I'd get a head start on the day." Okay, so she'd thought if she accidentally on purpose ran into Connor she could get a feel for what the hell was going on. She sucked in a few more lungfuls of oxygen and glanced at the clock. "Is Connor going to pick you up soon? I, uh, needed to ask him something."

The muscles along Kaleb's jaw tightened—he'd been so huffy the past few days. He shook his head. "I knew this would happen." He pushed out his chair and put his hands on her shoulders. "Faith, Connor is a player."

She tensed. "I know."

"Do you? He's a good guy, and my best friend, but he's not the kind of person who has relationships, and I don't want you getting hurt."

She thought about after their swim, when he'd told her he'd try, and how after the gas station she'd thought about letting him. But Kaleb's words made the part of her that still ached over the last guy who'd hurt her rise up, reminding her that she'd never been a no-strings-attached girl, and that most of her strings had been slashed, the edges now painfully frayed.

"He's a cop, too. Late hours, tons of stress. It's a bad idea to get attached all around. Just get through your time here, and then go do your internship in Charlotte. Okay?"

A knock sounded on the door and Kaleb glanced at it, then back at her, eyebrows raised. The same look he used to give her back in high school when he'd taken over being the parent.

"I heard you."

"Good." Kaleb headed to the door. Faith stayed in place, wanting a glimpse of Connor and not wanting one at the same time. Her heart quickened, but the open and close was too fast.

It wasn't like Kaleb told her anything she didn't know.

But the fact that he made sure to warn her about it only reiterated that it was true.

Since today was the day for setting up hay bales in the park, Faith contemplated forgoing a shower and just getting dressed in work clothes. But her muscles ached, she was sweaty, and she needed to take a few minutes under the steam to try to clear her head and convince herself she wasn't disappointed that she and Connor's whatever-it-was got stopped before it really even started.

She heard Ella playing in her room and tiptoed past before her niece could bombard her with requests to play dress-up or get her milk or put in a movie. She gathered her clothes and darted across to the bathroom.

A few minutes into her scalding-hot shower, Faith heard Ella crying.

I'll go help entertain her in a minute. See if I can't give Anna a break. Faith wasn't sure how Anna did it day in, day out, especially now that she was pregnant. Even with the water pouring full-blast, Faith could still hear her niece— man, that girl could screech like a banshee. She gave up on the long-shower idea, quickly got dressed, and followed the sound of crying.

Ella stood in the hallway in front of her parents' bedroom, her eyes and cheeks red from crying.

"What's going—" Faith's stomach bottomed out when she spotted Anna tucked into a tight ball on the carpet. She dropped to her knees and put her hand on her sister-in-law's shoulder. "Anna?"

"Something's…wrong," Anna wheezed, holding her stomach. "I need you to take me to the hospital."

Faith nodded. "Of course. Let's go."

"Take Ella next door. Mrs. Ferguson will watch her while we're gone." Anna looked at her crying little girl. "You're gonna go play next door and Auntie Faith's gonna take me to the doctor. Mommy's going to be just fine, okay?"

Ella nodded, but the tears kept flowing. Faith scooped up her niece and ran her next door, explaining the situation to Mrs. Ferguson as quickly as she could without scaring Ella. But under her calm facade, her blood pressure was rising and icy-black fear was wrapping itself around her heart. The baby wasn't due for five more weeks. If Anna was going into labor already… Faith swallowed past the lump rising in her throat, not letting herself think about that. Right now, she needed to be strong for Ella, and for Anna.

As soon as she got back into the house, she helped Anna to her feet. Her skin was pale and clammy and beads of sweat formed across her forehead. Faith wrapped her arm tighter around Anna's waist and got her into the Jetta. She tore out of the driveway, speeding toward the hospital. She called Kaleb's cell, but he didn't answer, so she left an urgent message.

Anna winced and doubled over.

"Is the baby coming?" Faith asked.

"I don't know. It feels like it."

Faith had never been great in a crisis—no, she tended to flip out. She wished Connor were holding her hand, giving her his strength, the way he had the other day. But he wasn't, so she took a deep breath and forced all the assurance she could into her voice. "Everything will be fine. The doctors will know what to do."

Anna gave a sharp cry, and when Faith glanced at her, she saw the blood on Anna's gray sweatpants. Her heart dropped, and she gripped the wheel tighter. She clenched her jaw to hold back tears. "We're almost there. Just hold tight a few more minutes."

Faith turned into the ER entrance. From there it was a blur of getting Anna checked in and nurses putting her in a wheelchair and taking her to a room. Once Faith got the chance, she called Kaleb again.

"Why isn't he answering?" she asked aloud, her breaths coming faster and faster. She didn't know how to handle this. He should be here. She scrolled through her phone, glad she'd kept Connor's number in her contacts despite her brain telling her she should've deleted it, day one.

The second she heard his voice on the other line, she burst into tears.

. . .

Connor pulled over the squad car, holding up a hand when Sullivan started to ask what he was doing. So far, all he knew was it was Faith, and she was crying. He turned up the volume on his phone so he could hear her better. "What's wrong?"

"It's Anna," Faith said. "I think the baby's coming, but I don't know, and I'm in the emergency room, and I don't know what to do, and is Kaleb with you because he's not answering and—"

"I'll be right there." Connor glanced in the rearview mirror, made a U-turn, and headed for the hospital. Of all the days for him and Kaleb to split off. He'd figured they both needed a break from each other after the tension between them the past few days—he'd seemed especially irritated this morning, even though Connor had done as he asked and left Faith alone. So he hadn't complained when he got to the station and Kaleb told him he was riding with Johnson today. But now he wished his usual partner were sitting in the seat next to him.

"Get on the radio," he said to Sullivan. "See if you can get ahold of Fitzpatrick."

It seemed to take him forever to get to the hospital, though Connor knew it'd only been a few minutes. Sullivan said he'd keep trying to get ahold of Kaleb and let him know what was going on. Apparently he and Johnson had responded to a boat accident out on the lake, where signal was hit-or-miss.

Connor flashed his badge at the security guard and looked around the waiting area. He didn't see Faith, so he went to the window and asked the nurse for information. She told him they'd moved Anna to a room, gave him the number, and pointed the way. Connor rushed down the hall, his pulse pounding through his head. His chest tightened when he spotted Faith's blond hair. She was leaning against the wall, her head down.

How was he supposed to stay away from her when all he wanted to do was pull her into his arms and never let go? He reached out and put his hand on her shoulder. "Are you okay?"

She turned her tear-streaked face up to him and a pang went through his gut. "They're hooking up monitors to the baby now, and I...I just feel so helpless." She sniffed. "Then I start crying, and I worry I'm only making it worse for Anna." A lone tear escaped and rolled down her cheek.

Connor would be the first to admit he didn't have a clue what to do when girls started crying—he pretty much ran in the other direction whenever one of his sisters did. He wiped away the tear with his thumb and tried to sound as reassuring as possible. "They'll take good care of both of them."

Faith threw her arms around his waist and hugged him tightly, burrowing her face into his chest. He squeezed her back, his emotions going in a hundred shattered directions. He always enjoyed their verbal sparring matches, watching her cheeks redden with anger. But this... Suddenly all he wanted to do was protect the girl in his arms and make sure nothing bad ever happened to her again.

He rubbed his hand across her back. "Everything's going to be okay."

"How do you know?" she asked, her voice muffled against his shirt.

He gently rested his chin on the top of her head. "I just do," he said, though what he was thinking was, *Because it has to be.*

When Kaleb came charging down the hall about thirty minutes later, he looked completely wrecked, face pale, hair sticking up at odd angles. A pang went through Connor, Kaleb's sorrow automatically transferring to him, too.

"She went into preterm labor, but they've put her on medication to stop the contractions," Faith told him as he approached. "And they gave her a steroid shot to help the baby's lungs, just in case she delivers early. She seems much better—she's sleeping, actually—and the baby's heartbeat is strong."

Kaleb threw his arms around Faith. "Thank God." He turned to Connor. "Thanks for coming down. And for making sure they got ahold of me." He gave him a quick hug with a hard slap on the back. Then he pushed through the hospital door, off to check on his wife.

Connor scrubbed a hand over his face. This day felt twice as long as any other. "Need a drink? Anything?" he asked Faith.

"I'm already beyond wired, so caffeine's probably a bad

idea. Water would be nice, though."

"On it." Connor tracked down a vending machine, got a couple of bottled waters, and headed back. Faith was staring off into space, and he took a moment to study her. Even with red eyes and tear-streaked cheeks, she was so pretty his heart ached to look at her.

He handed her one of the bottles and took the seat next to her. He didn't feel very helpful sitting out in the hall, waiting for more news, but he wasn't going to leave unless Faith asked him to. And that little baby in Anna's stomach was his nephew, too, even if not by blood.

Faith reached over the wooden chair handle and grabbed his hand. "I'm glad you're here." He was trying to come up with something genuine and not lame to say when she leaned her head on his shoulder, the smell of her shampoo or perfume—something that smelled so good he wanted to hold it in forever—hit him.

He'd resigned himself to leaving her alone and letting her live her life, like her brother asked him to.

But sitting there, her hand in his, he knew it was too late to go back now.

• • •

Faith slowed the car as she neared Connor's house. A headache was working its way across the top of her head and every muscle in her body ached from the long, physically and emotionally exhausting day.

"Don't drop me off," Connor said from the passenger seat. "I want to make sure you and Ella are settled in, then I'll walk home."

If she didn't feel like she'd fall apart at the lightest breeze, she might argue. Right now, though, she wanted to hold onto Connor and never let him go. Just the way he'd hugged her in the hospital—all those hard muscles wrapped around her in the softest way... Her heart swelled thinking about it.

She drove past his place, parked her car in Kaleb's driveway, and then she and Connor headed over to Mrs. Ferguson's to pick up Ella. The older woman swung the door wide and smiled. "Good to see you, Mr. Maguire."

"You, too, ma'am. I noticed the tree out front's been trimmed. Weren't you supposed to call me when you needed that done?"

Mrs. Ferguson swiped a hand through the air. "I know you're busy, so I hired someone. They weren't too expensive."

Connor leaned his hip against the doorframe. "I work for cookies. You can't tell me they gave you a better deal."

"Oh, you," the lady said with a giggle—was there no one the guy couldn't charm? Mrs. Ferguson tipped her head toward the couch, where Ella was fast asleep. "Little thing's all wiped out. How's her mama and that baby?"

Faith rubbed her aching neck, counting the seconds till she could get off her feet. "They're going to keep them overnight, make sure everything's okay. And it sounds like she'll be on bed rest for the remainder of the pregnancy."

"Well, if you need help, just holler."

"Thank you," Faith said.

Connor went to the couch and lifted Ella into his arms. She automatically curled around him, her eyes fluttering for a moment before going still again. Faith waved at Mrs. Ferguson, walked the short distance to Kaleb's, and opened the door. When she turned, her heart melted into a puddle. The combination of Connor, all strength and officer of the law, and Ella, her pink dress puffing out around his forearms and her blond curls flowing down over his elbow, was too much.

"Are you going to let me by so I can get this princess to bed, or what?" His voice was so deep she could feel the vibrations through her core. Seriously, how was she supposed to resist that? Her tongue was sticking to the roof of her mouth, leaving her incapable of words, so she simply stepped aside. She followed him down the hall, watching as he placed Ella in bed.

He pulled up the covers and kissed her forehead.

And Faith's ovaries exploded, she was sure of it.

She turned off the light and stepped into the hall. She could hear Connor right behind her. Feel the desire coursing through her veins. When she spun around, her chest knocked into his.

Connor's hands came up on her waist and that thin band of resistance that'd been pulling tighter and tighter between her and this guy since he first showed up in her life snapped. Her hands drifted up his arms, across his firm shoulders.

His eyes locked onto hers, passion swimming in the gray depths. But he didn't make a move—with the exception of his fingers digging into her waist tighter, proving he was affected by their nearness as well.

"I'm considering making a mistake right now." Faith swallowed, her throat so dry it felt like she'd choked down cotton. She slowly tipped onto her toes, sliding her hands behind Connor's neck and linking them there. Then she leaned in and brushed her lips across his.

He groaned when she pulled away, and a thrill shot through her. She lightly placed her lips on his, not pressing…

Yet.

The next thing she knew, she was against the opposite wall, and Connor's mouth was on hers. His body held her firmly in place as he forced her lips apart with his. He increased the pressure and tempo, fanning the flame of her desire until her sense of time and gravity slipped into a black hole of pleasant dizziness.

He gently bit at her bottom lip and then sucked it into

his mouth, before switching to her top lip. And just when she was breathless and unable to hold up her own body weight, he pulled back. A complaint was on the tip of her tongue, she was still blinking to get her bearings, and he spun her to face the living room instead of him. He smacked her on the butt and said, "That's what you get for teasing me. Now, let's order some food. I'm starving."

Starving? Are you freaking kidding me?

Then he walked past her, down the hall, as if the kiss hadn't affected him at all.

• • •

Connor stuck his hands in his pockets and clenched his fists, shaking from adrenaline and being so turned on he could hardly walk straight. Even as he moved toward the living room, he wondered if he was making the right move.

It was the *mistake* part that got to him. If he threw her over his shoulder, took her into the bedroom, and peeled off all her clothes with his teeth like he wanted to, she'd forever think it was a mistake. Probably even blame her vulnerable state.

No, he wasn't going to let her get away with that. He wanted to show her they had more than chemistry, although *holy shit*, did they have chemistry. He dug his fingernails into his palm, telling himself not to think about that right now, because he'd need to turn and face her eventually. He started running through the Miranda rights in his head. *You have the right to remain silent.* He often wished people would, though they rarely did. *Anything you say or do may be used against you in a court of law.*

Speaking of this being used against him, Kaleb was going to be pissed. But the way Faith had looked at him earlier, like he was the hero she'd been waiting for—how was he supposed to resist that? He wanted his lips against hers again, her bare skin under his fingertips.

Focus, Maguire.

You have the right to consult an attorney before speaking to the police and to have an attorney present during questioning now or in the future.

Another deep breath, and he was under control again. He pulled out his phone and flopped onto the couch. "What do you like on your pizza?"

Faith's eybrows drew together, and he could feel the frustration coming off her. Her lips twisted in that way they did when she was annoyed at him. "Everything. And make sure you get double onions."

He ordered the pizza exactly like she'd requested, never letting his smile drop. Then he sat back on the couch and patted the spot next to him. "Come 'ere."

She crossed her arms. "I don't respond to 'come 'ere.'"

He shot out his arm, gripped the waistband of her shorts, and yanked her to him. She fell onto his lap and he kissed her hard on the mouth. "I want you. I've wanted you from the moment I saw you in the bar. But I'm not a mistake. And until you get that through your pretty head, I'm not sleeping with you."

Her mouth dropped open. "Seriously? All your innuendos and flirting, and now you're saying no?"

"I'm saying not yet." He moved his lips to her neck, dragging them across her soft skin to the spot under her ear. She was trying to keep an unaffected front, but her shallow breath gave her away. "Not when you're only doing it because you've had a rough day."

Something in her seemed to break, and— *Oh shit, she's going to cry again.* If this was what he got for trying to be sensitive to how she was feeling, he might have to reassess this plan of attack.

She moved off his lap onto the couch cushions and let her head fall back. "You're right. I'd only feel better for a little while." He was about to break in and say that it'd be a *long* while, but stopped himself when he saw the tears gathering in her eyes. "When I saw her on the floor, and the blood—but she's okay. The baby's okay." It seemed like she needed to say it aloud to know it was true.

Connor took her hand and brushed his thumb over her knuckles. "They're both going to be fine. You did a great job getting there in time."

She nodded, over and over, almost on autopilot. "And we can deal with bed rest. I can watch Ella and do the cooking, cleaning, and whatever else she needs." Her determined expression faltered. "Except for... Well, I don't really know how to take care of a kid full-time. She cries a lot, and I usually hand her over to her mom when that happens. I'm good at nail-painting and makeup, but I don't know when she eats or what she eats or how to make sure she eats."

"Don't worry. I'll help. We got this."

"We?" she asked, turning her eyes on him.

And now he was thinking he was an idiot for not taking things further all over again. He leaned down and gave her a gentle kiss on the lips. "We. I'm gonna help you, Blondie."

After a moment she exhaled a long breath. "Okay, I'm sure I'm gonna need it. And Kaleb can tell me how to take care of Ella. Anna, too. I'll ask her to write out instructions and schedules and such when she can."

Connor wished she hadn't brought up her brother. He wanted to be the vailant guy who always did the right thing, but he also wanted to be the guy who got to be with Faith, and right now, those two things seemed to be at odds. Maybe he could show Kaleb that he could have a long-term realtionship with her. A twinge of panic shot through his chest—that was a lot of pressure, and he didn't normally think about the future, not like this.

He only knew something had been missing in his life, and whenever he was around Faith, it went away. But she was his best friend's sister and one of his heroes' daughter—she couldn't be a hookup, and if things didn't work out, it would be a big deal, not something he could easily walk away from. But before he got carried away, he needed to focus on one day at a time. Tonight, he wanted Faith to know everything was going to be okay and prove he was interested in a real relationship.

She leaned her head on his shoulder and everything inside him turned warm and squishy. "You're a good guy when it comes down to it, Connor Maguire."

Holy hellfire, he'd never been so turned on by a woman saying his name.

"Don't get me wrong, your ego's still way too big. And your pickup lines are just awful..." She tilted her head up and flashed him a smile. "But I guess you're not a complete meathead."

He laughed. "Any more compliments from you, and I don't know if I'll be able to recover my ego."

"I'm not worried. You've got quite a backup supply."

He curled her into him and leaned back against the couch cushions, enjoying the little sigh that escaped her lips as she used his chest for a pillow. He wondered if she could hear how hard his heart was beating. They were both nearly asleep when the doorbell rang and their damn double-onion pizza arrived, making him curse himself again for mentioning food in the first place.

Chapter Eleven

Faith was glad she and Connor hadn't gone too far last night. She was. Totally.

She wasn't still contemplating why he put her to higher standards when he clearly had no problem with casual sex. Or wondering if it would've been as good as she thought it'd be, considering she'd never gotten quite that carried away with a kiss before.

"Auntie Faith?"

Faith sat up in bed, squinting against the harsh light. It was the second time Ella had come into her room this morning—if four a.m. was considered morning. She thought it qualified as night still, AKA the time when people should be sleeping, but Ella had needed chocolate milk and the bathroom and she couldn't find her princess doll and couldn't they do makeup again?

The day had barely begun, and Faith wanted to go back to bed. But she needed to be there for her niece, as well as Anna and Kaleb. So she was going to be the best babysitting/cooking/whatever-she-needed-to-do-to-help auntie ever.

"How 'bout we start with breakfast?" Faith asked, clapping her hands to try to get herself excited as well as Ella.

After pouring Ella a bowl of Lucky Charms, Faith glanced out the window at the lake. *Crap. How am I supposed to go for my run when I can't leave Ella?* Mrs. Ferguson had offered to help, but Faith didn't want to abuse the offer, and she supposed it wasn't like she'd be able to drastically improve her time all that much over the next week and a half anyway.

Faith glanced at the kitchen, noticing how dirty it was. She'd used the last of the milk for Ella's cereal, which meant grocery shopping was at the top of the list—hadn't they just gone shopping? She shook her head, refocusing. She decided to start on the dishes.

"Morning," a deep male voice said, and she dropped the bowl in her hand. It hit the sink and broke apart.

Faith put a hand on her rapidly beating heart and looked over at Kaleb. "I didn't know you were here. Scared the crap out of me."

"Sorry, I just came in." He pulled his shoulder blades together and his back cracked. "Sleeping in a chair all night was rough. Didn't actually get much sleep."

"How's Anna this morning?"

"She's feeling a lot better. The doctor was going to swing by and check her, and then they might let her come home. But she's under strict orders to stay in bed. The first thing she said was, 'But I can't miss the festival. Surely I'll be better by next weekend,' and the doctor told her it wasn't an option, even if her contractions stop. So she's bummed about missing it after all of her work to get the park and her pottery ready for it, but she realizes it's not worth hurting the baby." Kaleb leaned against the counter and rubbed at his bloodshot eyes. "Thank you for taking care of her yesterday. And Ella."

Faith dropped the broken bowl in the trash under the sink. "Of course. Whatever you need, just let me know."

"I could use a few more hours of sleep if that's okay. Connor texted to say he took care of covering my shift, so I won't have to go back into work until tomorrow. I know Ella's a handful, though, so if you need he—"

"You go rest. I got this."

• • •

Faith *so* did not have this. Ella had leaped out of the cart onto her three times, slamming her forehead into Faith's chin on the last one. Faith kept buckling her in, but the dang kid knew how to Houdini her way out, no matter how tightly she belted her in.

At least she'd made sure everything was in place for the festival with some help from the other members of the committee—they might've been slacking lately, but when they found out about Anna, they'd called an emergency meeting and divvied up everything left on Anna's to-do list. Of course Mrs. Lowery had volunteered Faith for several things, and when she'd asked who they should give Anna's booth spot to, Faith had said not to give it away. That she'd be selling the pottery for her sister-in-law.

Faith's phone chimed with a text. It was Connor, responding to her earlier text asking if he could help haul the pillars, pop-up tent, and pottery to the festival.

Sure. Whatever you need.

She let out a breath. At least that was taken care of. Except she still wasn't sure how exactly it'd work. She stared at the screen and then made an impulse decision.

Come over tonight so we can figure it out? I'm making dinner. It was probably a bad idea, especially since Kaleb had told her to forget about Connor just yesterday. But that was before Anna was put on bed rest. In order to pull off taking over the pottery booth last minute, she'd need help—Kaleb would understand that. She might have to resist the urge to kiss Connor again, but she could do that.

She was relatively sure.

I'll be there as soon as I get off work.

Faith grinned and glanced at Ella. "We better find something good to make for dinner. Good, but easy." She pushed the cart to the next aisle and grabbed a jar of Alfredo sauce. When Ella started to stand, Faith held her in place with one hand while reaching for a box with the other. "How do you even know which damn kind of pasta you need?"

"Damn!" Ella yelled, gaining the attention of everyone. The nearby adults glared at Faith, channeling their disdain straight into her with their frosty stares.

Of all the words she'd said, why did Ella pick up that one? Faith changed her mind about the macaroni pasta, and decided to go for the cute bowtie ones.

"You really shouldn't let her stand like that," a woman said as she neared, her child sitting in the front, eyes glazed over like she'd been plied with Nyquil.

Is it okay to do that? Not that she would, but she got how it might be tempting.

Ella was standing again, her foot propped on the handle of the cart, because Faith had let go of her for two seconds. "Sit down," Faith said and her niece grinned and sat down. Faith's arms ached from everything she'd done today, which made her feel like a total wimp, but after scrubbing the house and catching Ella approximately one hundred times, she was tired and wanted to get the shopping done and get out of here.

Faith surveyed the ingredients in her cart. She'd spent most of her college years living off take-out and ready-made food. She supposed now was as good a time as any to learn how to cook. How hard could it be?

• • •

When Faith swung open the door, warmth flooded Connor's chest.

"She hasn't slept," Faith said instead of offering a greeting. "In fact, she hasn't stopped moving since this morning. She took a permanent marker to the bathroom and to her face. I tried to scrub it off, but she's so squirmy, and that's before you add water and soap. I think I got more water on me out of the tub than she did in it." Faith ran a hand through her hair and kept it on top of her head. "She doesn't stop."

Connor stepped inside. "Where's the little tornado now?"

"Probably destroying something, but I don't want to know, because she's not crying and she's locked in the house, so at least there's that."

Ella sprinted into the room, her curly hair matted and blue marker covering her arms and cheeks. She ran toward him and he lifted her and tossed her in the air. She giggled and squealed, "Again!"

Faith's eyes followed the motion and then she sighed. "I don't know how I can do this day in and out for the next month or so. I suck at it."

Ella giggled and wrapped her arms around his neck. He made a funny face at her and she clapped her hands, asking for another one.

Faith frowned. "Seriously, how are you better at taking care of her than me?"

He should be offended, but he could sense her exasperation. "One, I haven't been with her all day, and two, I'm used to it. Just imagine four more running at you at once."

Faith's eyes widened so large he had to bite back a laugh. He wrapped his arm around her waist, hooking his hand on her hip. "You've got this. And now I'm here to help, so put me to work."

"If you've got the rug rat, I'll start dinner."

Connor took Ella to the kitchen and got her Goldfish

crackers, tossing back handfuls as he watched Faith move around the kitchen.

"So," Faith said, "today I was thinking…"

Connor perked up, hoping she was about to finally give in and admit she liked him.

"Kids are so much work," Faith continued. "If she were a wolf, she'd be hunting age by now. If wolves can figure it out, surely we humans can think of something."

Connor glanced at Ella. "You wanna be a wolf?"

Ella howled.

"Looks like she's good to go." He raised his hand and Ella gave him a high five. Then she used her nose to scoot crackers toward him. He picked up a couple, but she put her hand over his, stopping him from lifting them to his mouth.

"Wolf. See." She ate her crackers off the table without using her hands.

Connor glanced at Faith, shrugged, and then ate the Goldfish off the table. He was pretty sure there was jelly mixed in there, too, and he had no idea how old it was. Faith smiled at the two of them, and he winked at her. Her smile grew, bringing out the slight dimple in her cheek. The stress of the day seemed to fall off her, and Connor couldn't wait until he got to kiss those perfect lips again.

She lifted a box of pasta, squinted at the back, then leaned down to get something out of a cupboard. Her shirt rode up as her pants lowered a couple of inches. A tiny swirled four-leaf clover peeked out on the right side of her back. How did he miss that the night they were swimming? Probably because it'd been dark and he'd been focused on the front of her body. On most girls, a tattoo was hot. On Faith, it was so unexpectedly hot that he tipped back his chair and ran his finger across it. She jerked up and shot him a look over her shoulder.

And all it did was made him want to kiss her more.

An Irish girl with an Irish temper, though? He worked hard to keep his temper in check all the time, careful to always stay in control. He'd come close to losing it on a few cases—the Corbett one included. He didn't want to ever use his temper as an excuse, the way Dad used to. Instead, he learned other ways to get out his frustrations, like running and lifting. But with how stubborn Faith was, and with how easy it was to get into arguments with her, he'd have to watch himself even more. Always be under control.

Suddenly he was questioning if dating her was a good idea all over again.

His chair legs came back down, jolting him harder than he expected. He'd barely recovered when he was pelted in the side of the face with orange crackers, a couple of them nice and slimy. Faith laughed and then covered her mouth with her hand. But it was too late. Ella thought it was hilarious and launched another attack. She tossed a handful at Faith before he could take away the ammunition.

Ella screeched, big tears forming in her eyes. He picked her up and she wailed right in his ear. He tossed her in the air and caught her, but it didn't work this time. So much for being good at this.

"I think she's cranky, since she refused to take a nap," Faith said. "See, if she were a wolf, I bet she'd put herself to sleep."

Ella didn't howl this time—well, not like a wolf, anyway. The tears and wailing escalated. But he could feel her body slacken in his arms. He gently pressed her head to his shoulder and bounced her. "I'll see if I can't get her to fall asleep."

Connor moved into the living room and hummed. When it seemed to relax her, he went ahead and sang "Stella Stellina," a song his mom used to always sing, and still used on her grandkids when she was trying to get them to drift off.

A couple weeks ago, he would've laughed if someone told

him this would be his idea of a great night. But he pictured Faith in the kitchen, cooking, and it was so much better than another meal at the Rusty Anchor or even grabbing a beer with the guys. And if he could get this tired little girl to fall asleep, he might actually get a couple of minutes alone with the woman who'd been on his mind since the minute he woke up that morning.

...

The guy was singing a lullaby in a different language—Faith was pretty sure it was Italian. Seriously? How was she supposed to resist that? It was like someone mixed all the right ingredients for the perfect guy. If only they didn't leave out fidelity. Maybe that was unfair. She kept comparing the way he'd admitted to not being good at relationships to the way Jeff had said basically the same thing, as if she could sift out the truth from the lies if she focused hard enough.

Connor's back was to her, and Ella's eyes drifted farther closed with every bounce and word of his song. A tingly mix of attraction and affection pumped through Faith's veins. Usually she worked to keep her emotions calm—on the surface, at least—but lately they were rising up, impossible to hide. Especially around Connor. He'd helped her out a ton this week, proving there was much more to him than good looks and charm. But she worried she was relying on him too much, growing too attached.

She'd feel better taking a chance if Kaleb hadn't warned her away.

Still, she'd never experienced such an intense connection in such a short amount of time before, and he didn't dance around the truth like Jeff had. He told it to her straight, from his attraction to her to his lack of relationship skills. He'd definitely be an adventure, if not a happily ever after.

The hiss of water hitting the burner interrupted her thoughts, and she rushed back to the stove. The pasta water was frothy and spewing over. "Crap." She turned down the burner and read the instructions again. She'd done exactly what it said. The Alfredo sauce was boiling, large bursts splattering over the pan, onto the stove. She moved it off and frowned when she saw the bottom half of the chicken in the other pan was beyond brown, much closer to black.

Wasn't blackened chicken a dish, though? She'd just pretend it was supposed to be that way. She slid the pieces into the Alfredo sauce—at least she knew it'd be good, since she'd bought it instead of attempting to make it from scratch. Why go to all that trouble when Ragu had done it for you?

Faith combined all the ingredients in a large dish and stirred around. "Looks pretty good if I do say so myself."

Her cell rang, and when she saw Kaleb's name on the display, she answered. "Are you guys on your way? Dinner's almost done."

"Thanks so much, but Anna's blood pressure shot up, and they want to keep her one more day for observation, just in case. I know Ella's a handful," he said.

"It's fine. Don't worry about us," Faith said, though she was worried how she was possibly going to survive another full-time day with Ella. But she was more concerned for Anna and the baby, so she'd suck it up and do whatever it took, despite the fact she'd been dreaming about going to bed since about four in the afternoon.

"Anna's feeling pretty down, so I'm going to sleep here again. I'll be by early in the morning to get dressed for work. Unless you need me there now. Like I said, I know Ella's a handful."

"Actually..." Faith didn't want to upset Kaleb—and without him coming home, he'd never know—but it was stupid to hide things from him. "Connor's over now. He's trying to get Ella to fall asleep. With his help, I'll be okay."

With every second the line remained quiet, her stomach hitched higher. Why did she feel so nervous? She was an adult, free to make her own decisions. "Tell him I said thanks," he finally said. "I do feel better knowing he's there."

"He's really good with Ella."

"I know."

He's really good with me, she thought, which was silly but true. Maybe if she accepted Connor as more of a for-now guy, instead of pressuring him or herself to make it into something more, she could keep her heart from getting broken. A summer fling. People had them all the time. Who knew if they could actually get along for long enough to pull off a relationship, anyway?

She told Kaleb to keep her updated, disconnected the call, and opened a bag of salad mix. As she was finishing setting the table, Connor came in, his hands free.

"You got her to sleep?" Faith asked.

Connor rubbed his hand across his jaw and nodded. "She's out like a light. For how long is anyone's guess."

Faith filled him in on Anna and Kaleb and then they sat at the table to have dinner, just the two of them. Suddenly she was afraid to make eye contact, like he'd sense she'd decided to have a summer fling with him and attack her.

Then again, I might kind of like for him to attack me, she thought, her cheeks heating.

Connor made a choking noise. He reached for his drink and drained it in a couple of large gulps. Then he set the glass down and looked across the table at her. "Wow, that's..." He wiped the back of his hand across his mouth and shook his head. "You're sexy and funny and can talk trash like nobody's business. But you can't cook for shit, babe."

All her happy, tingly, I-wanna-start-something-with-this-guy vibes vanished. "Ah! I'm never cooking you dinner again!"

He reached across the table and covered her hand with his. "Don't be mad. I'm sure you'll get the hang of it. Or we'll just be one of those couples who eat out all the time—that works for me."

She yanked her hand free. "You can go by yourself, you jerk. And don't call me 'babe.'"

"Okay, sexy."

She clenched her jaw, and all he did was grin at her, amusement flickering in his eyes. "I notice you haven't tried it," he said, pointing his chin at her plate.

Faith picked up her fork and shoved a bite of pasta in her mouth to prove it wasn't that bad. Connor was watching her closely, so she tried to chew and act like it wasn't the worst thing she'd ever tasted in her life. The noodles had coagulated to one gooey yet crunchy chunk, and the overpowering charred taste made it clear she'd burned more than just the chicken. Come to think of it, the pasta sauce was more brown than white. She held back a shudder as she swallowed. Connor pressed his lips together, obviously working hard not to laugh.

Faith grabbed her glass of milk and took a large drink to wash it all down. "It's..." She dropped her fork and sighed. "How am I going to do this for a month and a half? I can't take care of Ella without losing my patience, can't get her to go to sleep, and I can't cook dinner."

Connor's face softened. "Hey, it's not *that* bad. I just wasn't expecting... Well, it's raw and burned at the same time. It's a lot of...flavors to deal with. Now that I'm prepared..." He wound noodles around his fork and started to lift them to his mouth.

Faith put her hand on his wrist. "It's disgusting. Don't eat it."

The fork clinked against his plate as he released it. "I'm

sure the salad is good. I'm always thinking I should eat more vegetables." He dished himself a large helping and passed it over to her. Luckily, the company who bagged it knew what they were doing—after the burned food it tasted especially amazing, although not very filling.

"About taking care of Ella," Connor said, his eyes locking on Faith's. "The fun part of being the aunt or uncle is coming in, playing with them, and then getting to leave. It's one thing to deal with whining or tantrums for an hour or two. It's another thing to do it all day. You'll get the hang of it, though." One corner of his mouth twisted up. "And we'll work on the cooking thing."

After they ate their salad and a lot of bread, they cleaned up the disastrous kitchen. When Connor moved to wipe off the counter in front of her, he caged her in with his arms and pressed his body against hers. Then he leaned down and kissed the back of her neck. A hot flush spread from his lips to her core.

"Connor," she tried to say, but it came out with little air behind it.

"Yeah, babe."

She twisted to face him. "If we're gonna do this—"

"We are," he said, closing the mere inches between them and causing the point she needed to make go wispy.

She swallowed, her heart thumping hard in her chest. "You've helped me a lot in the past few days. I appreciate it, and I do...care about you." It felt like her skin was too tight all of a sudden, so she rushed on with the rest. "But I know you don't normally do commitment, and I think it'll work better for both of us if we agree from the start that it's not serious. We're not... This isn't like a relationship."

Connor lightly kissed her lips. "If this isn't 'like a relationship,' I'm not sure what a relationship is."

"You know what I mean. We don't have to be exclusive.

Like if you want to go out with someone else, you…can. No big deal." The words tasted bitter on her tongue, like the little lies they were. Yes, he could, but it'd hurt her, despite telling herself she could handle it if she knew it were a possibility instead of getting surprised with it.

Connor dropped the rag he'd been using and pulled her flush against him. "If you decide to go on a date with another guy, you'd better make sure he's bigger and tougher than me." His snarky eyebrow raise made it clear he didn't believe that were possible. "Because I'm not going to just watch that happen."

"You're threatening my hypothetical date?"

He kissed her deeply, sliding his tongue in to meet hers and claiming every inch of her mouth. He tilted her head back and looked her in the eye. "I'm saying, you're mine, *babe*. And this isn't *like* a relationship, it is one. So get used to it."

She needed to argue—a guy like him didn't change overnight, she knew that. And she was trying to find the words. But then his lips came down on hers again, he pressed his hips into her, and words just seemed so damn unimportant.

She gave in to the kiss and he boosted her onto the counter. His hand slid up her leg, to the hem of her shorts, her skin burning every place he touched.

"Mommy!" Ella's voice was filled with tears. "Mommy!"

Connor leaned his forehead against the cabinet behind Faith, his breaths sawing in and out of his mouth.

"I got it," Faith said, the rise and fall of her chest matching his. She kissed his cheek and scooted off the counter. Ella stood in the hallway outside her parents' room, tears streaming down her face.

"Mommy," she said with a sniff.

"I know. She'll be home soon, okay?" Faith lifted Ella and her niece wrapped her arms around her neck. Faith glanced over the curls at Connor, who looked slightly disheveled, like he might have run his hands through his hair a couple times—maybe even splashed water on his face.

He sat on the couch and Faith carried Ella over to sit next to him. Then they fired up *Sleeping Beauty* and settled in for what was most likely going to be a long night.

Chapter Twelve

Faith heard Ella's tiny voice, followed by a much deeper one. Her brain was still in the foggy half-asleep stage, and judging from the odd angle of her neck and the kink that might never go away, she guessed she'd slept on the couch.

"She's being Sleeping Beauty," Ella said. Nice, but probably an exaggeration considering Faith's hair was usually a tangled mess in the morning.

"And how do you wake up Sleeping Beauty?" Connor asked, and Faith's heart rate steadily increased, chasing away the last of the haziness.

"Tiss of tourse."

Connor's heavy footsteps crossed to her and she bit back a smile. His breath fanned her face and then he pressed his mouth to hers. "Wake up, Sleeping Beauty." His words vibrated against her lips and traveled down her core.

Faith kept her eyes closed. "What if you're not my prince?"

"Then you'd still be asleep." He kissed her again, running his tongue across the seam of her lips. Suddenly, she was feeling very awake, and remembering how they'd been interrupted last night.

When she opened her eyes, she was greeted with the image of her dead-sexy cop, uniform and all. Ella stood next to him, a chocolate-milk mustache and the remains of the unwashable blue marker on her face.

"I put Ella to bed around three, and considered carrying you to your bed." Connor leaned closer and lowered his voice. "But I wasn't sure I could keep myself from only setting you in it, and I was afraid your brother would catch me in there and kill me." His lips brushed her ear, sending goose bumps skating across her skin. "Right now, I'm thinking it would've been worth the risk."

Faith ran her hand down Connor's cheek, noticing it was smoother than last night. "You shaved."

"I snuck back to my place to take care of Penny and get ready for work. Kaleb got home about an hour ago, and he insists on going in today, even though I told him the guys and I could take care of it."

A door opened and closed in the hall, and Kaleb came into the room, dressed in his uniform.

"Uncle Connor woke up Auntie Faith with a tiss," Ella said, and Kaleb's shoulders tensed.

Connor patted Faith's thigh and shot her a tight smile. "Looks like my day is gonna be interesting." He stood and readjusted his belt. "Are you sure you don't need me to get your shift covered again, man? I don't mind."

"No. It looks like if I take off a day, everyone will forget the *simple* instructions I gave them."

Faith glanced from Kaleb to Connor, back to Kaleb. They were having some weird showdown, and she didn't like feeling out of the loop, especially when it obviously involved her. "So, um, I appreciate the protective vibe and all, Kaleb, but I can make my own choices, you know."

"It's just that I remember who you always turn to when your choices end badly," Kaleb said, "and I don't have time to take care of anything else right now. I've got my hands full as it is."

Offense pinched her gut. "I can take care of myself."

"Like when you ran out of gas?"

"That could happen to anyone," Connor said, and he and Kaleb went back to staring each other down.

Faith stood, putting herself between the two of them and addressing Kaleb. "I'm trying to help you. I want Anna to get well as much as you do, and I'm doing everything I know to do. I wish I was better with Ella; I've just never done this before. But I'll figure it out, I swear."

Kaleb sighed. "I know. I'm sorry." He ran a hand through his hair. "I don't know what I'd do without you here." In that moment, he turned from the guy who'd always protected her, to a guy on the verge of cracking under everything going on in his life. "But I still worry. I need both my sister and my best friend if I'm going to get through this, and it'd be easier if I didn't feel like killing one of them." His hardened gaze went back to Connor.

Connor opened his mouth, but Kaleb threw up a hand. "We need to go, or we'll be late. And I'd rather Ella not hear this discussion anyway." He bent down and kissed Ella's cheek. "Be good for Auntie Faith, okay? And if Mommy can't come home this afternoon, I'll take you to see her."

Ella's lower lip trembled. "Mommy."

Kaleb put his hand on Faith's shoulder. "Call if you need me." He jerked his chin toward the door and Connor glanced at her for a moment before he followed. As hectic as her day with Ella was sure to be, she thought that Connor might have it worse than she did.

• • •

As Connor walked toward the squad car, he told himself whatever happened next, getting to kiss Faith had been worth it. More than that, though, she'd needed him—even admitted it, out loud—and he never realized how nice it was to be needed on that level. It was deeper than his job, and when she'd told him she cared about him, the shell he'd kept around his heart for so long cracked open and filled with her. There was no going back now, and he'd fight for her if he had to.

"I can't tell you how much I appreciate what you've done for my family this week," Kaleb said. "But this thing with you and Faith will only end badly, and it pisses me off that even when I told you *why* I didn't like it, you blew it off."

Connor got into the passenger seat. "I tried, man. But she called me, and what was I supposed to do?"

"Keep it in your pants."

"Technically, I did. So far, there was just ki—"

"I don't wanna know. I don't suppose asking you to stop would do any good?"

"I'm not gonna lie to you, man. I can see where you're coming from, but I already care about her. I'll treat her right, I promise."

Kaleb shook his head, his jaw set, and fired up the car. The thick silence settled over them as he pulled onto the road.

Connor readjusted the radio so it wouldn't come loose if they hit a bump, and for something to keep his hands busy. After another minute of silence, he cleared his throat. "I was even thinking, with her career, Faith'll know how to handle my line of work better. If things get that serious."

"Shit," Kaleb said. "You've actually thought that far ahead? You really are serious."

"I told you I was."

"Did you tell her how you knew my dad? About why you became a cop?"

Connor swallowed. It'd taken six months of knowing Kaleb before he'd even told him exactly why Officer Fitzpatrick was one of his heroes and what the man had done for his family. "I told her he was one of my heroes. I'm not quite ready to tell her the rest—not because I'm not serious, but hell, we haven't even gone on a date yet. I'd like to at least take her out and get to know her before I start sharing my sob story."

Kaleb slowed for a stop sign. "I still don't like it. But… you better take her out somewhere public, not your house, and if you hurt her—"

"I get it."

"I don't think you do. I've felt responsible for her ever since I can remember, but even more after my dad died. I've ended up hating every guy she's ever dated. It'd be a shame to lose my best friend."

The pressure pressed against him, like when he was at the gym and got cocky with too much weight and no spotter and he wasn't sure he'd get the bar off his chest before it crushed him. Risking himself for work, even putting the side of himself out there that he usually hid, he could handle that—if only he got hurt. But being with Faith meant risking his best friend, on top of knowing he might accidentally hurt her, even though it was the last thing he wanted to do. Usually, he'd say it wasn't worth it. He kept picturing her face, though, and thinking about how she saw through his bullshit and always had a witty comeback. Her passion for helping people and that damned awful pasta that somehow only made her more adorable.

If anyone in the world was worth the risk, it was Faith. "I promise I'll take care of her."

Kaleb didn't say anything. But his hard glance and stiff posture said, *You'd better.*

· · ·

By lunchtime, Faith couldn't take it anymore. She needed to at least check in with Connor. She sent him a text.

You still alive? Missing any limbs?

A few minutes later, he texted back. *Any particular limb you interested in?*

She shook her head, cool relief washing over her. If he was joking, he must be just fine. She was trying to think of a good comeback when another text came in.

Got permission to take you out this weekend. There are lots of rules attached, but it looks like you'll finally get that hot date you've been begging me for since the night we met. A second later. *Stop shaking your head. You know you want me.*

Ella whimpered, holding up her sandwich, speaking what Faith was pretty sure was an alien language made of high-pitched squeaks. Flirting when a toddler was in the room took multitasking skills she wasn't sure she had.

Faith moved toward Ella but kept her eyes on her keypad. *Actually, just realized I sent this to the wrong number. Pardon me while I text my other too-cocky-for-his-own-good guy.*

Tracing your texts now. Other guy will be out of the picture momentarily. And seriously, that's not funny.

Ella pointed at the crust on her sandwich and Faith realized that Anna normally cut it off. So Faith removed the brown edges and gave the food back.

Partner is giving me dirty looks for texting on the job. See you later, BABE.

A flutter went through Faith's chest, and instead of stopping herself from enjoying it, she leaned back and basked in it. So she'd failed horribly at resisting a ridiculously hot guy who knew how to calm her fears and handle a two-year-old. A few weeks ago, she'd had no idea how amazing those qualities were.

"Cannonball!" Ella leaped off her booster chair, narrowly missing the counter. She giggled and grinned up innocently.

"Kid, you're gonna give me a heart attack."

Ella tore off down the hall, most likely to destroy something, and Faith made a mental pros and cons list about letting her do it. Pro, she'd be happy and out of her hair for a moment. Con, she'd have to clean it up later. Pro, it might make her tired enough to take a nap.

And the pros win.

Faith turned to wash her hands and noticed a scrapbook poking out from under the pile of bills on the counter. Mom used to spend hours scrapbooking, always putting all their pictures in colorful books with stickers and clever word bubbles. Faith tried to help once, but got bored about five minutes in.

She tugged the book out from under the bills, her heart squeezing when she saw the familiar blue fabric and the family photo of her, Kaleb, Mom, and Dad. Faith had a similar pink book, but it was buried in the boxes she'd stored instead of unpacked every move. She sat down at the kitchen table and opened the book, instantly transported to past memories. On Lake Norman, fishing. The Christmas she got an Easy Bake Oven—clearly that hadn't made her a good cook. In fact, now that she was thinking about it, she'd only ever burned brownies in it.

The McAdamses were in several of the pictures. Page after page of fishing, each fish documented. There were a couple of other candid snapshots, Dad still in his uniform, since she and Kaleb often attacked him the second he got in the door, climbing over him and insisting on rides. He always gave in, too, regardless of how tired he must've been.

Ella ran back into the room, a doll tucked under one arm—upside down and an inch away from falling to the floor—and a princess wand in the other hand. "Dat book has grandpa. He was a cop, dust like Daddy." She yanked down the book and pointed. Then she took off in the other direction, her doll's head dragging against the floor.

A moment ago, Faith had been excited thinking of a date with Connor—of forgetting her reservations and allowing herself to see where it went. Now all she could think was *he's a cop, he's a cop, he's a cop.*

The summer fling idea was stupid, but pretending she could have a long-term relationship with Connor Maguire— or that she could keep herself from falling for him—was even stupider. The guy was quicksand, drawing everything to him, no escape once you got in too deep, and she was one more good night with him away from letting him suck her under.

Maybe I should cancel our date. Tell him something came up.

Knowing him, he wouldn't accept a text excuse. And she wasn't sure she could go through with canceling if she heard his voice.

· · ·

Connor wanted to be over at Kaleb's house, helping with Ella, sneaking kisses with Faith, and making sure everything went smoothly with getting Anna back home. But right as Connor had been about to leave for the day, Sullivan tracked him down. Erica Corbett's neighbors called in, telling the dispatcher they'd heard shouting.

So he found himself in front of an all-too-familiar door with Sullivan, clenching his fists as he waited to see who'd open up. Waiting to see if Erica would have bruises on her face, or if her asshole of a husband made sure he hurt her in places clothing would cover.

"Don't lose it, dude," Sullivan said. "One more outburst

and the sheriff will take you off the case for good."

"I know. I'm in control." Honestly, he was never fully in control at any domestic-disturbance call, but he knew how to play the game. He'd come pretty damn close to taking a swing at Hal Corbett when they'd taken him in last time, but Kaleb had talked him down. He'd scared himself enough that he'd gone over it later, pinpointing when he'd started to lose it so he could keep from doing it again.

Connor raised his fist to knock again and Erica Corbett opened the door. Clearly she'd been crying, her eyes and cheeks red and wet with tears. "We got a call from a neighbor. Said there was yelling."

"It was just a small fight, Officer Maguire. I'm fine, I promise." She smiled, but it was shaky, no joy behind it.

"You know I'll help you," Connor said, lead filling his gut as the sensation of being out of control and bad memories tugged at him. "You say the word and I'll make sure he never touches you again."

Erica glanced over her shoulder, eyes wide, and Hal appeared behind her a moment later.

"What's the problem, Officer?" the little shit of a man asked, his smug grin needing to be wiped off his face with a nice hard punch.

Angry heat built low in Connor's stomach, rising through his chest, pumping through his veins. He sucked in a breath and held it, counting down from ten in his head.

"Noise complaint," Sullivan said.

"Everything's fine." Erica's eyes met Connor's. "We were just watching the game and got carried away cheering. We'll keep it down. Thanks for stopping by."

In his mind, Connor saw himself yanking the door open and showing the man who abused his wife exactly how it felt to be beat by someone larger. Deep breath in, long breath out. Sullivan glanced at him and he gave a small nod, so the guy knew he was okay. "We're going to be patrolling this neighborhood all night, making sure everyone's nice and safe."

"Thanks, Officer," Hal said, taunting him with another snake oil smile. "I really appreciate it."

With little else they could do, Connor walked back to the car with Sullivan. "You can go home if you want," Sullivan said. "I'll drive by a few times after I drop you off."

Connor eyed the house, watching for movement inside. One of his biggest fears was finding out Erica was in the hospital this time—or worse. He kept hoping he'd get through to her. He wondered if Faith could help somehow, using what she'd learned. Maybe he could convince Erica to meet them away from the house. He knew it was easy to give up on people like her, but he also knew what could happen when one person out there didn't.

Someday she'll be strong enough, and I'll be there when it happens. "Nah, I'll ride with you for a while longer. It's probably too late to go see my girl now anyway."

"Don't you mean girls?"

Connor shook his head. "I'm done with that. I'm with Faith now."

Sullivan burst out laughing and then clamped his lips when Connor shot him a glare. "Fitzpatrick's cool with you banging his sister?"

Connor reached over and smacked the back of his head. "I'm dating her." Sullivan's eyebrows drew together, confusion etched across his features. He didn't care what the guy sitting next to him thought—Connor had been guilty of not understanding before. But he wasn't about to get into why it was different this time, or how Faith made him want more. "Just shut up and drive before I take my anger out on you."

Sullivan put the car in gear and muttered, "Jeez, someone gets pissy when he's not getting laid."

"Hey, without me in the picture, you might actually have a chance now."

Sullivan flipped him off and started the car. As they pulled away from the tiny gray house, Connor glanced at the glowing windows, the light cloaking the darkness within. The pinch in his chest happened every time a call went this way. Usually, he'd go hit the weights to push away the sense of failure and the bad memories that always followed. Instead he focused on Faith, and how things were finally changing between them.

His phone rang and he smiled when he saw Faith's name. "There's my girl now," he said, liking the sound of it even better the second time. Right now, having a girl to call his felt like the only thing getting him through the day.

Chapter Thirteen

Faith had meant to cancel her date with Connor, she truly had. Only when he'd answered the phone, his voice held such happiness and hope and a vulnerable undertone that made her think he'd had a rough day. Then he asked how she was holding up, and they'd ended up talking and laughing over the phone until she started to fall asleep, his calming voice in her head.

The next three days, she went back and forth between "it's okay to go out with Connor" and "it's the worst idea ever." But mostly she'd been busy checking on Anna now that she was home, making sure she didn't overexert herself, and taking care of Ella and last-minute things for the festival. She'd hardly stopped to take a breath and she was desperate to get out. And, well, Connor showed up looking like himself, and her hormones screamed louder than her rational thoughts.

Connor leaned in and pressed a gentle kiss to her lips. "Hey, Blondie." Kaleb cleared his throat from his spot on the couch. Ella sat next to him, her eyes glued to *The Little Mermaid*—a nice change from *Sleeping Beauty* three hundred times a day, actually. Anna was back in her bedroom with mac and cheese Faith hadn't messed up by some miracle and access to a boatload of movies.

Connor took Faith's hand and laced his fingers with hers, meeting Kaleb's gaze head-on. A wordless conversation passed between them, then they said their good-byes and Connor led her outside.

Faith stared at the giant black Silverado with raised tires, shaking her head as he opened the door for her. "You would drive something this huge."

Connor put his hands on her waist. "Stop acting like you're not impressed with my huge everything, and get in." He boosted her onto the seat and gave her knee a quick squeeze before closing her door. The cab smelled like him, earthy and woodsy and whatever sexy smelled like.

Even in this huge truck, he seemed to take up all the space. When he slowed for a stoplight, he glanced at her. His eyes darkened and a shiver of anticipation trembled across her skin. He leaned over her, his hand skimming her leg as he reached to the other side of the seat and grabbed the lever.

And then her seat was reclined all the way back. He crushed his lips to hers, a quick, hard kiss, and then she shot upright again, the seat clicking into place. The light turned green and he accelerated through the intersection, a huge grin on his face, while she worked on catching her breath.

"Pretty smooth," she said.

"Right?" His hand curved around her thigh and heat pooled low in her stomach. For the entire drive to Charlotte, she went back and forth between excited and nervous, for both the date and the fact that the date involved a helicopter. She was trying to pretend she wasn't a bit worried about whatever adventure he'd planned. As they were pulling up to the helicopter office, though, she cracked. "This is going to be mild, right? Like my mild, not yours."

"Don't worry," Connor said, which made her do the opposite of what he said. "Most girls wouldn't appreciate where I'm taking you, but after the way you talked about going with your family the other night..." He twisted the keychain in his hand. "Well, I figured it'd be better than me trying impress you with an expensive meal at a fancy restaurant."

Faith couldn't help staring. She loved how confident he was, but the slight waver as he went over tonight's plan tugged at her heart. "As long as we're not jumping out of the helicopter, I think I'll be okay." She leaned over and kissed his cheek. "I don't want the lady-killer treatment."

He draped his arm around her and curled her closer, brushing his nose against hers. "Well, that's not something I can just turn off." He sighed dramatically. "It's a blessing and a curse."

"I'll try to control myself."

"I'd rather you didn't." He nipped at her bottom lip and then took her hand, pulling her out of the truck on his side. Like the show-off he was, he hefted the large backpack he'd brought onto one shoulder, never letting go of her hand. All those muscles, the grin, taking her fishing—resistance was futile.

Dani and Wes met them inside the office and then they climbed into the helicopter. Faith's stomach rose as they did. The ride was smooth, and the scenery passing under them beautiful. About thirty minutes later they were touching down in a meadow somewhere in the Blue Ridge Mountains.

Wes pulled off his headphones and shut down the helicopter, the sound of the blades slowing until everything went quiet. He pulled what she was pretty sure was rappelling gear out of a compartment in the helicopter.

"Um, are we rock climbing there?" she asked, eyeing Connor. "'Cause that's not mild."

Connor squeezed her hand. "Wes and Dani are going to climb one of the smaller falls once we get there. You and I are just fishing."

Wes shoved the gear into a large black backpack. "Unless you want to climb? I have enough gear in the helicopter."

"By a slippery waterfall?" Faith shook her head. "I'm good with just fishing, and you know, not breaking all my bones."

"It's not that slippery," Wes said to Dani when she raised an eyebrow at him. "Definitely easier than that climb we did in Bald Mountain, even with the water."

Dani shook her head. "The things you talk me into."

"Five bucks I can make it to the top before you."

She looked at him, a competitive glint in her eye. "You're going down, Turner." He held out his hand, she put hers in his, and they started into—well, the wilderness. Like the kind you needed a machete to get through.

Connor wrapped Faith's hand in his and they followed after them. She thought maybe they'd come across a trail at some point, but it was just Connor and Wes consulting their compasses, occasionally saying to head a few klicks north or west. Hopefully they knew what they were doing, because Faith couldn't find her way back to the helicopter if her life depended on it. The three of them looked like they'd done it several times before, though, so she tried to keep up even though her legs were shortest by far, ducking low-hanging branches and climbing until her thighs and lungs burned.

After an intense forty minutes of hiking, as Connor was giving her a hand over a large rock, she asked, "Is there really not a nice, easy trail to get to the lake?"

"There is, but…" The trees suddenly cleared and there was a stream leading into a cave with a waterfall cascading through it. The sunlight coming through a hole in the top of the rocks illuminated the spray of water, turning it into glittery drops against a dark background. The contrast gave the entire place a cinematic, magical, almost too beautiful to be real feel. Connor laced his fingers through hers. "Then we'd miss this."

They stepped over slippery rocks, sticking to the higher ones to avoid getting their shoes too wet, and entered the cave. Droplets sprayed off the rocks, hitting Faith's cheeks and every spot her skin was exposed. Connor wrapped his arms around her waist, pulling her back to his chest.

For a moment, she simply stared at the beautiful scene before her. Then she glanced over her shoulder at Connor. He lowered his lips to hers, and she turned, never breaking the kiss and tugging on his shirt, pulling him closer. He grinned against her mouth and wrapped a strong arm behind her back. She inhaled the mix of him and the water, taking a moment to enjoy the warmth of his mouth on hers and the cool water splattering her skin.

When she pulled away, she noticed Wes and Dani enjoying a moment of their own. She'd never really double-dated—definitely not in the extreme adventure way. But it was nice, seeing the friendship between them and Connor, having them accept her so easily. Being here with a guy of her own that she knew could and would take care of her.

They headed across the cave and she noticed the light growing. Water trickled over the rocks, dripping into the lake at the bottom of the slope.

Dani peeled off her jacket to reveal a Lycra tank top and peered up to the very top of the rocky wall, where the water started. Wes was pulling out climbing gear, the two of them working like they'd done it a hundred times.

Wes glanced at his watch and then Connor. "Catch you back here in about two hours?"

"Have fun." Connor put his hand on Faith's back and they started down the slope. The ground leveled out and Connor took off his backpack. He unrolled a raft, sticking in a pump and setting it to fill up. Then he assembled the oars. Faith saw the fishing poles in the pack, so she took them out and put them together, going so far as to put PowerBait on the hooks.

Within a few minutes they were pushing off into the calm blue water, toward the afternoon sunlight fanning out in the distance. Connor rowed them out in long, powerful strokes, his muscles working in a way that was hard not to watch.

Faith pushed against the side of the yellow raft. "I've actually never been in a blow-up boat. I keep getting the image from the cartoons where it pops and goes skidding across the water for a few seconds before sinking."

One corner of his lips kicked up. "There are separate compartments to keep that from happening. Even if one popped, I'd be able to get us back to shore before we started to sink."

Faith reached over the side, into the water, watching tiny green floaties swirl around. After several days watching a two-year-old who never stopped moving, she drank in the peace and the chance to close her eyes without being afraid something would need to be done—or worse, ruined—when she opened them.

"So, how've the past few days been?" Connor asked.

"Yesterday I tried to wear Ella out by chasing her around the yard all morning, but the only one exhausted was me. She was still jumping around like she'd downed a six-pack of Red Bull. Which made me think, hey, I should start drinking Red Bull to keep up. Only that'd require going to the store, and I didn't think I'd have enough energy without the drink, so it was a bit of a catch-22."

Connor flashed her a devastatingly handsome smile.

"Today I had a semi-breakthrough, though." Faith paused her story to cast, the familiar *plunk* sound in the water small, yet comforting. "I found out she actually loves to help, so if

I can keep her busy, she's less likely to destroy something or leap on me when I least expect it. Then we tapped off the day watching *Sleeping Beauty* two times in a row, during which I fell asleep and she gave me this—" She swept her hair aside and showed him the purple marker spider on her neck.

Connor set the oars down and leaned in to study it.

"I woke up to Ella telling me there was a spider on my neck, so of course I jumped up and started screaming, trying to get it off me."

Connor laughed, a deep, rich sound that sent happy ripples through her chest. He kissed her unwanted spider tattoo and the mix of soft lips and stubble on his jaw made her heart skitter. "Sorry, the past few days at work were crazy. I told you I'd help and then I couldn't get over there."

She slowly let her hair drop, peering into his eyes now that he was so close. "It's okay. I'm glad I haven't had to call you freaking out. Hopefully that means I'm doing something right."

"You're doing a great job." After days of being tired and worrying she was doing everything wrong, it was exactly what she needed to hear, and it made warmth spread through her chest. Connor trailed his fingers down her arm, making the heat spread to her skin, too, and gave her hand a quick squeeze. Then he cast his line, the boat gently rocking.

When they'd first met, she was working so hard to push him away, making assumptions about him, and she suddenly realized there was a lot about him she still didn't know.

"Did you grow up here? In Cornelius, I mean?" He was older than she was, and there were plenty of people in the area she didn't know, but with his killer good looks, she assumed she would've heard girls talking about him before.

"Spent my childhood on the other side of town, but I moved to Huntersville when I was in high school."

Faith thought he might expand on that, but he didn't.

"Is your family still in Huntersville, then?"

"My mom is. Everyone still lives close, though. Got a sister in Charlotte, one in Hickory, and my brother's in Gastonia. We get together at my mom's place about once a month." He glanced at her. "This Friday they're celebrating my graduation from the SWAT program, actually."

Faith flinched. It was easy enough to forget about the SWAT thing when they were painting in the park, watching a two-year-old together, or flirting over the phone. Even the cop aspect she was trying to swallow, but the fact that he and Kaleb were who'd get called if anything bad in the area went down? She didn't like thinking about it at all.

"You should go with me."

Faith was stuck on the SWAT part, so it took a moment to realize he meant he wanted her to meet his family. At least she thought that was what he meant. "Go with you where?" she asked, not wanting to make a fool of herself if she'd drawn the wrong conclusion.

"To my mom's for the party. I want you to meet her. It's one of the few days I have free, and I want to spend it with you and my family."

Yet another thing about Connor that was the opposite of Jeff. She'd finally met his mom once, but it was brief, and the woman didn't even act like she'd heard of Faith before. Connor seemed to jump headfirst into everything, but he had to know that this was a semi-big step in most relationships, right?

"If I go with you, your family's going to think we're really serious."

"How many times do I have to tell you? I'm serious about you."

"But there's serious, and then there's *serious*."

Connor smiled and tipped his head, amusement crinkling the corners of his eyes. "You think too much."

"You don't think enough."

His grin only widened and then he tugged her to him, capturing her mouth with his, their fishing poles forgotten between them. She wanted to hold onto her argument, but her body reacted automatically, clinging to his. She parted her lips, letting his tongue slip in to meet hers. With every stroke, it was harder to remember what they'd been talking about. The boat swayed and Connor tightened his grip on her. He slid his hands to her butt and boosted her onto his lap so she was straddling him. Energy crackled between them and she ran her hands over the curves and indentions in his arm muscles. She rocked her hips and he groaned into her mouth. His hands slid up her back, under her shirt, pressing her closer. Dizziness set in, heat zipped through her veins. Delirium was seconds away, but she couldn't help the pesky thoughts that were tugging her the other way.

She kept thinking about his job. The long hours, the risks he took every day. She wasn't sure it was something she could just get over. Letting go completely was so tempting, but she remembered how much it hurt to lose someone she cared about in such a devastating way.

"You're thinking again," he said, and she realized she'd pulled back. Her breaths were still shallow and her body still burned every place they were connected.

"I have a brain. It doesn't just shut off."

He pressed his forehead against hers. "Just give me a shot, Faith. I won't let you down, I swear."

As she stared into his eyes, his fake charm stripped away, she saw a guy who was sincerely asking her for a chance. Her heart clenched, a riotous mix of fear and attraction pumped through her veins, and she thought that a relationship-minded Connor might be even more dangerous than the player one.

• • •

Connor didn't know what had gotten into him, but he needed to hear that Faith would give him a chance. He'd never felt this way before, and he didn't know how to do it except go all in.

"I..." Faith put her hand on the side of his face, her fingertips soft against his skin and her green eyes wide. "Not thinking things through has gotten me hurt before. And your job..." She swallowed and her voice wavered. "It scares the hell out of me. *You* scare the hell out of me."

There were a lot of things he was willing to do to convince her he could be with her and only her, but his job was who he was. It was how he righted the past.

"But..."

His heart skipped a beat at that *but*.

Her fingertips dragged across his jaw and his breath lodged in his throat. "Well, let's face it, I totally failed at staying away from you. And you know I already care about you. So...I'm in."

Happiness uncurled in his chest and he leaned forward to kiss her. She leaned back just before his lips made contact. "But..."

He liked this *but* less than the last one.

"I might need some time before we move past kissing. I'm sure you're used to going faster, but I don't want to get hurt again, so I'm trying to be more careful this time. I'd like to get to know you better first. Actually date a bit and that kind of thing."

"Okay." He smiled down at her, glad it wasn't nearly as bad as he'd thought it'd be. "So that probably means I should get my hand off your fine ass and get back to fishing."

One corner of her mouth twisted up. "Probably."

He kept it there for a beat longer, giving it a gentle squeeze that made her jerk and shoot him a dirty look so cute it should be illegal. For this girl, he could be patient, even if it meant he'd also be frustrated every second he was around her. Between how she first reacted to him and cared about who he'd slept with, to what she'd just said and what Kaleb had told him, he was guessing the last guy had cheated on her—idiot bastard. He figured the only way to prove he wouldn't do the same was show her over time.

He untangled himself from her, gave her a quick peck on the lips, and moved back, taking up his fishing pole again.

"About the party with your family. If you still want me to go...I'd like to meet them."

He did want. He knew it'd bring up questions. Faith would no doubt ask about his dad, and he'd need to tell her the whole story eventually. But that wasn't enough to keep him from wanting to take her home with him. Plus, he couldn't wait to see the priceless look on his mom's and siblings' faces. "I'd like that."

He scooted sideways so he could be closer to her, and she turned so they were side by side, looking out over the glimmering water. She leaned her head on his shoulder and his heart expanded until it pushed against his rib cage.

This girl was already his.

Even if she didn't know it yet.

Chapter Fourteen

On the drive to Huntersville, Faith chewed on her fingernail, contemplating the dangers of opening the door and rolling out. She wasn't sure what it was about meeting Connor's family that had her so tied in knots, but it was like her subconscious knew nothing would ever be the same again. Only she didn't know if it'd be a bad thing or a good thing or—

Connor put his hand on her thigh and rubbed his thumb across her skin, calming her and causing her heart rate to skyrocket at the same time. "Relax, baby." His fingers brushed across her skin again. "I approve of the dress, by the way. I told you how sexy you looked, right?"

"That's what I took the opened-mouth 'damn' after you looked me up and down to mean."

He squeezed her thigh tighter, and she was so turned on that at least the fear of meeting his family was more background noise now. "My family is going to like you. It'll be fun, you'll see. You can hold my hand the whole time, and if anything bad happens, I'll be there to provide mouth-to-mouth. I'm certified and everything." He shot her a butterfly-inducing grin.

Last night they'd taken Ella to McDonald's so that Kaleb and Anna could have some quiet time at home. While she had thought having a toddler around and being in public would keep her from forgetting she and Connor were going slow and jumping him, she found that every game he played with Ella, every time he pulled her into his arms, she was only more attracted to him, and it wasn't like he needed any help in that department. Honestly, whenever she was around him, she'd start thinking about the way he kissed her, how he looked shirtless, and how he would look with even less clothing on. Yes, she'd been attracted to guys before, but she'd never felt so one-track-minded.

I wonder if this is what it's like for guys all the time.

Considering Connor's fingers were straying higher and higher, she had a feeling it was the same for him anyway. She eyed the heavily wooded side of the road and seriously thought about telling him to pull over—screw going slow, she was over it. But then they'd be late to his family gathering, and she'd no doubt look like she'd had sex. This meeting was going to be hard enough without adding that.

"So…" She worked to steady her voice. "You've got two sisters, one brother, and did you say five nieces and nephews?"

"Right. Don't worry if you can't get all the names and faces matched—I still forget half the time." He grinned at her and then his smile faded. "I also need to tell you…my parents are divorced. My dad won't be there. He won't ever be there."

There was a dark edge to his voice and the muscles in his jaw went rigid. Obviously he had issues with his dad. The psychologist in her wanted to know what had happened, but she also knew that he needed to share it in his own time. Still, she couldn't help asking, "You want to talk about it?"

"Not yet." He glanced at her. "I want you to meet my

family and get to know them first. Is that okay?"

Like that night on the phone, she got the sense that he needed her. Even if it was only moments here and there, she wanted to help him the way he'd helped her. She covered his hand with hers. "Of course."

For the rest of the drive, she simply enjoyed being next to him.

Only then he pulled up to the house and she started regretting not rolling out of the truck a couple of miles ago. Her stomach crawled up to her throat as Connor led her to the front door. His fingers curled around her hand as he pushed through the entry.

The buzz of conversations filled the air, but as soon as she and Connor stepped inside, all talking stopped, and there were at least a dozen eyes on them. Connor walked toward the beautiful older woman standing in the middle of the room—the same woman from the picture he had on his side table—and kissed her cheek. "Hey, Mama."

He nodded at the others—his brother and sisters from the photo, though they were a little older. There were also two guys who must be Connor's brothers-in-law because they didn't look anything like the rest of the family. "I'd like you all to meet Faith Fitzpatrick."

Faith raised a shaky hand. "Hi."

Connor wrapped his arm around her waist. "Faith is Kaleb's little sister. And she's also my girlfriend," he said, and Faith's stomach did a somersault. He pointed out everyone by name and she tried to keep them straight. Honestly, they all looked a little shell-shocked, to the point it was almost comical. Obviously he didn't bring many girls home.

He really is serious about me. A lightness filled her chest, despite her nerves. He'd told her, sure, but actions spoke so much louder than words, and as much as she wished she didn't need that reassurance, she did.

A dark-haired little boy ran in from the backyard and his eyes widened. "Uncle Connor's here!" he yelled and then four other kids came running. Connor tossed them all in the air, one by one, and within a few minutes, the room was buzzing with conversations again.

His sisters and brother came over to congratulate Connor on graduating from the SWAT program. They included Faith in the conversation, asking her about what she did and other get-to-know-you questions. His mom came over last. She took Faith's hand and patted the top of it.

"It's so nice to meet you, Faith." Nicola glanced at Connor, adoration filling her large brown eyes. She stared at him like he was her baby and her hero, all at once. It sent an overwhelming burst of longing for her own mom through Faith. In a lot of ways, having Mom withdraw from life so much after Daddy died felt like losing both parents at once. Mom was a little better now, and they called back and forth, but Faith still worried about her.

Nicola turned to Connor and patted his cheek. "I'm so proud of you, *mio bambino*." She switched to Italian, and the only other word Faith caught was *bella*.

Connor winked at Faith. "She certainly is *bella*." His mother said something else, and he replied, "I will."

"Now let's eat," Nicola said.

Faith tugged Connor back as the rest of the crowd headed into the dining room. "What did she say?"

"She said she was happy I finally found someone, and that you were beautiful. Then she told me to make sure I treated you right."

Faith wrapped her arms around his waist, tipped onto her toes, and kissed him. "I like that plan."

He lowered his mouth to hers, lingering for long enough to make the room spin. Then he laced his fingers with hers and led her into the kitchen. There was so much food covering the table, Faith didn't even know where to begin. As soon as she took her first bite, though, the flavors bursting in her mouth, she decided she could never cook for Connor again. Not when he'd grown up eating food like this.

As loud as it was with so many people crammed in one tiny room, kids jumping up and down, the love and energy flowing through the room made her want to kick back and stay a while. Possibly forever. Even though Connor was younger than his sisters, he checked in on them, his sense of responsibility for them similar to the one Kaleb had for her.

Through it all, Connor would check on her with an eyebrow raise, hand squeeze, or smile. The out-of-control sensation she often got around him moved to the background, fading more every time he pressed his hand to her back or pulled her into conversation with one of his family members. With every passing minute, she fell a little harder.

On her way back from a bathroom break, she studied the pictures in the hallway. There was one of the kids and she moved closer, squinting at the smiling boy in the middle. He had Connor's features, but—

"He used to be the cutest little chunk, no?"

Faith turned to Nicola. "I never imagined him as a little kid before." He *was* a chunk, too. Not just round in the face, but chubby all over.

"He was always so sweet. So protective. Still is."

Connor appeared in the entrance of the hallway. His face fell as he glanced from his mom to Faith to the picture. "Oh no."

"I was just telling Faith what a sweet little kid you were."

"I was a not-so-little kid."

"You were always my handsome boy," Nicola said. "Still are."

Red colored his face—he was actually embarrassed! Faith shouldn't enjoy watching him squirm as much as she did. She thought she'd seen all of Connor Maguire's shades of hotness, but this was a different level entirely. In that moment, she saw the little boy in the picture.

"Okay, Mama," he said. "That's enough embarrassing me."

Nicola planted a big, smacking kiss on his cheek and then walked back toward the kitchen. Faith stayed in front of the picture. "You were a cute kid."

"I was chubby. My mom kept feeding me dishes of pasta meant for three people. She still tries to fatten me up every time I come over."

"Well, last time I checked, you didn't have an ounce of fat on you, so I think you're good."

"You wanna check again? Just to be sure?" He tilted his head toward an open bedroom door, his signature cocky smile back on his face. He wrapped his arms around her waist and pulled her to his ridiculously ripped body. "Luckily I discovered basketball in high school and signed up for a weightlifting class—I was sick of feeling weak. I got into shape, and after years of rejection, girls took notice. I suppose I used that to my full advantage."

"You suppose?" she asked, and he shrugged, a what-can-you-do shrug that shouldn't have been as hot as it was. "Now that I know you speak Italian, I'm surprised you don't use that. Don't you know how sexy it is?"

"I do just fine without speaking it—you're here, aren't you?" He brushed his lips across hers, aptly proving his point. "Plus, it's more…personal. I only really speak it around my mama, or my brother and sisters occasionally."

"I see," she said, curling her fingers into the fabric of his shirt.

"But…" He swept her hair off her face and placed his hand on her cheek. "*Se vuoi, te ne parlo.*"

The words wrapped around her and ratcheted up her

already rapidly beating pulse. She swallowed past her suddenly dry throat and raised her eyebrows.

"I said, 'If you want, I'll speak it to you.'"

Instead of answering with words, she used the grip she had on his shirt to tug him closer and kiss him. Footsteps sounded in the hallway, and the twin girls showed up, blinking their big eyes at Faith and Connor. Considering neither of them had kids, it was funny how often kids interrupted them.

As they headed outside so Connor could push his nieces on the swing set, he wrapped his arm around Faith's shoulders and said, "Thanks for coming with me today."

Now that Faith knew Connor better, she realized she was wrong ever thinking he was anything like her ex. She curled into him, hugging him tightly and thinking she never wanted to let go. "Thanks for asking."

• • •

Connor waved good-bye to his family and helped Faith inside his truck. He'd wanted her to come home with him so he could spend another day with her, show her off to his family, and so he could prove to her that he was all in.

What he didn't expect was to look at her and feel like he was getting ready to dive off a cliff, all the thrill, none of the fear. For the first time in his life, though, he worried about what would happen if there wasn't a pool of cool water waiting at the bottom of the dive. Maybe he'd hit the ground and never recover.

How could so much of how he felt be wrapped up in one person? Part of him thought he was stupid for avoiding feeling like this for so long, and the other part was glad he'd never lost his mind like this before. As tiny as she was, Faith seemed to take up the entire cab. She was part of his life already, one that couldn't simply lift out.

"What?" she asked, her cheeks coloring slightly.

He wanted her close enough to feel her body heat next to him, inhale her perfume, brush his fingertips across her bare skin. "Faith Fitzpatrick, would you please scoot over here so you're not so far away?" He patted the spot right next to him.

"Wow, being around your family turned you into a gentleman."

"You wouldn't be saying that if you knew what I was thinking."

She scooted closer and he wrapped his hand around her thigh—he decided it was an even better place for his hand than her back. Really, it was a win-win, though.

As he pulled onto the freeway, his lungs tightened. He could sense it coming, but it was like his body was trying to hold his past in, even though he'd decided to let it out. But it was time to tell Faith the full story. "The first time I met your dad was because I called the police."

Faith looked up at him and he wondered if he should take her to his place before he told her the rest. But he'd probably talk himself out of it, and at least driving, he could focus on the road instead of how talking about it made his chest achy and raw. Considering the hollow sensation in the pit of his gut, that theory wasn't holding up, though.

"Why did you call the police?" she asked.

"Because my dad hit my mom. He'd done it before—did it all the time. But it was getting worse and worse. She used to..." He blew out a breath and pushed through. "She'd tell us to go to our rooms when they started fighting. I guess she thought we wouldn't realize he hit her. But we all noticed the bruises. How she'd limp the next day."

He kept his eyes glued to the yellow, dashed line on the road and cleared his throat. "When I'd ask her about it, she'd give me money and tell me to take my brother and sisters to get ice cream. As you saw in the picture, I went out for ice cream a lot."

Faith put her hand on his knee. "Connor..." She seemed to be struggling for words.

"It's okay," he said, assuring her. Assuring himself. "Anyway, I was the oldest boy. It's not like my sisters could do anything—my dad didn't take back talk. He..." Connor gripped the wheel tighter. "He had a bad temper, and he lost it a lot. We were all scared, but as I got older, I kept thinking maybe I could stop him. One night I tried. He... Well, he was bigger than me."

Even after all these years, he didn't want to admit that his dad had knocked him out with one punch. Dad was so pissed about giving him a black eye, not because he'd hurt him, but because people would ask—he made Connor swear to tell everyone he got hit by a baseball and that he better sell it, or he'd never go anywhere again. As Mama tucked him into bed that night, even as she was holding her most likely broken ribs, she begged him not to interfere ever again. That she could take it.

Faith raised his hand to her lips and pressed a kiss there, so tenderly, he almost lost his fragile grip on his emotions.

He clenched his jaw until his teeth ached. "The next time I didn't step in, and I felt like a coward. So when it happened a couple months later, I snuck into the den and called 911. Your dad was one of the officers who showed up. I was so relieved when they took my dad away. But of course, my mom... She was scared. And all her family was in Italy and she didn't have a job. So she bailed him out and didn't press charges, sure he'd finally change. But he didn't. One day after school I walked to the police station instead of riding the bus home. I found your dad and asked him for help."

The headlights from another car lit up the cab and Faith's eyes were glistening. Shit, he didn't want her to cry. Especially since it made him feel like damn near crying, too.

"I'm sorry." The words scraped his throat on the way out. "This was a bad idea."

"No," she said, tightening her grip on his hand. "Connor, pull over."

He glanced around and found a turnoff a few yards up. He maneuvered the truck over and then parked on a deserted part of the road. For a moment, the cab of the truck was dead silent.

Faith unbuckled her seat belt and twisted to him. A tear had escaped and was slowly trailing down her cheek. "I don't know what to say. I could give you all the responses I've been trained to say, but it's about you and your mom, and then you tell me about my dad... I have no idea what to say, but I'm glad you're telling me, and I don't want you to stop. But I might cry. I can't help it."

Connor wiped the tear off her cheek with his thumb and she threw her arms around his neck. He hugged her tightly for a moment, inhaling her scent and breathing out the bad memories. "Your dad, he wanted to help so badly, and every time I called the police, he'd show up and say that they got a noise complaint from the neighbors so my dad didn't know it was me." This was the first time he'd told the story in so much detail. Even when he'd told Kaleb, Connor kept the details light. That Officer Fitzpatrick had helped him when Connor's father had abused his mother, not about the two-year struggle.

"One night Dad lost his temper with my sister, and my mom realized she had to do something to keep her kids safe. So she called the police. Turned out she'd also been documenting the abuse with pictures. Dad went to jail for a couple years, we moved to Huntersville for a fresh start, and I decided that someday I was going to be the cop who showed up and helped people who couldn't help themselves."

He exhaled. There. He'd gotten it all out.

Faith sat back and a couple more tears rolled down her cheeks. It felt like one word and either one of them might crack, and while it was good to get that off his chest—he never even discussed it with his family—he worried again that it was a mistake. "Kaleb knows my dad was arrested and that your father helped, but…I don't want him to know it all. I'm…I'm still ashamed I didn't do something sooner."

"You saved your mom. Your family." She placed her hand on the side of his face and locked eyes with him. "You should never be ashamed."

"Spoken like a true shrink," he tried to joke, but it didn't come out quite right. When she opened her mouth, that overly analytical expression on her face, he pressed a finger to her lips. "Thank you for listening, but I don't want to talk about it anymore. I need…something else to think about."

She nodded, then slowly leaned in. Her warm breath hit his neck seconds before her soft lips. He closed his eyes, focusing on the sensation. She trailed kisses up and along his jaw. She ran her fingers through his hair and his thoughts swam to a pleasant blur. Then her mouth came down on his. It was sweeter than most kisses they'd shared, but in this moment, it was exactly what he needed.

For a long time, he'd felt like something was missing in his life. Now he realized it wasn't something, but someone. And he hoped like hell that they'd figure out a way to work it out, because he didn't want to ever go back to the way life was before he'd met Faith.

Chapter Fifteen

By all appearances, nothing much changed. But inside, everything was changing for Faith. Every look that passed between her and Connor, every touch, made her fall that much more for him. And just when she thought she couldn't like him more, he'd run the 5K, then come back to where she was—right when she was ready to give up on running and walk the rest—and encouraged her to the very end, telling her that she was doing so well. That she was almost there.

She'd told herself it wasn't about her time—she was doing it because the money would go to support families of fallen heroes, a cause she strongly believed in. But when she crossed the finish line faster than she ever had before, a swell of pride filled her from the inside out. She'd jumped into Connor's arms and kissed him with reckless abandon, not caring about all the onlookers.

"Catch," Connor said now, lifting one of Anna's blue clay pots and swinging it toward her.

Faith jerked up her hands, to catch it if it came down to it and try to say stop all at the same time. "Dontthrowit!"

Connor laughed, not releasing the pot. "You really thought I was going to?"

"With you, I never know."

He placed the pot on the table in front of her, caging her in with his arms, and kissed the back of her neck. They'd both showered and met back at the festival to set up the tent and all of Anna's pottery. They'd made approximately one hundred trips to and from the van, so when a woman selling jewelry showed up with one bin and set up the booth across from theirs within a couple of minutes, Faith couldn't help feeling like she had it easy.

When all the pillars and plate stands were in place, the pottery on top of them, Faith took a picture with her phone and sent it to Anna. She stepped between the tents and took a picture of the park and gazebo all decked out, too, and she had to admit that today she was feeling a sense of pride being part of the Cornelius Fall Festival Committee, whether it'd actually been voluntary or not.

On her way back into the booth, Connor pulled her onto his lap instead of letting her cross to the chair next to him. Once the festival started, she'd have to move, but for now she relaxed back against him, shivering as he pressed a kiss to the sensitive spot under her ear.

Connor's mouth moved higher, his lips brushing her earlobe. *"Mi fai impazzire, bella,"* he whispered, and zips of electricity traveled across her skin.

A throat clearing interrupted the moment. Kaleb had Ella and was standing in front of the booth. Her poor brother was still adjusting to his sister and best friend as a couple. "It looks good." He set the phone credit-card reader on the table so they could take payments that way, and Faith slid onto her own chair so her brother didn't have to keep looking like he was going to have an aneurysm.

Ella leaned forward for hugs and kisses, and then started

pointing at all the booths with their balloons and bright colors. She tugged on Kaleb's hand, trying to get him to move.

Kaleb let her pull him a couple of steps. "Guess I'll take Ella around. Unless you guys need anything else."

"We're good," Faith said. "If you run across the cotton-candy machine, though, I wouldn't say no to some." She grinned extra-wide, and her brother shook his head, but she knew he'd bring her back a bag.

Throughout the day, a steady stream of people stopped by, a lot of them having come from all around the county. She noticed plenty of women giving Connor sex-me-up eyes, but he didn't give anyone a second look.

They'd steal kisses here and there, and Connor would whisper innuendos in her ear and pinch her butt about every time he moved past her—she'd almost dropped a plate the first time he'd done it. Anna's pottery sold well, piece after piece. Faith kept her updated to try to make her feel like she wasn't missing out on too much. Hopefully the money from her sales would help her feel better as well.

After they'd packed up for the day, Connor closed the van and crooked his finger at her. "Come 'ere."

Faith crossed her arms. "I thought we talked about this. I don't respond to 'come 'ere.'"

"I must've been paying too much attention to your pretty mouth to listen to what you said. Happens a lot, actually." He took a step toward her. "Did you just say you can't live without me?"

She took a step toward him. "You wish."

"Why yes, I'd love to make out with you. Thanks for asking." He slid his hand behind her neck and lowered his mouth to hers. He took his time, exploring every inch and holding her against him.

"Officer Maguire?" Mrs. Lowery approached the van. "You're not forgetting about your shift at the pie-throwing booth, are you?" Someone's grandma or not, Mrs. Lowery had the worst timing.

"I was just about to make my way over there." Connor took Faith's hand and they walked across the grass to the gazebo. The fresh paint and shingles looked great, the twinkling white lights strung around it showing off all the hard work and smashed pie.

There were several cops from the station gathered at the booth, watching Grant Sullivan get pies thrown at him. Connor kept his arm around Faith as he introduced her to the guys she didn't know. Kaleb came over, his hair damp and dressed in a different outfit than he'd been in earlier.

"I missed your shift?" Faith asked. She knew he'd taken Ella home a while ago, but she'd thought she might throw a pie or two at her brother. For charity, of course.

"Just got back from cleaning myself up. Mrs. Ferguson's staying with Ella and Anna, but I thought I should come and contribute. Get all of Anna's pottery and stands home and"—Kaleb slapped Connor on the back—"make sure my partner has enough people throwing pies at him."

Faith tried to gauge how the vibe between them was, but they were both so straight-faced she couldn't tell. Connor took the van keys out of his pocket and handed them to Kaleb. "Everything's in there. I'll get Faith home."

Grant came out from behind the board with the face hole and a cop uniform painted underneath it—apparently it was to remind people you were throwing pie at a cop, while not risking staining their uniforms. Connor stuck his face through the hole. All of the other activities from the festival were slowing down, so a crowd was gathering to watch the final cop get pelted with pies.

Kaleb went first—and his aim was dead-on. The other guys from the station cheered and jeered, while other people laughed and Faith hoped it wouldn't result in a fistfight later.

Kaleb came down the steps and moved over to Faith. He let out a long exhale. "I feel much better now, actually."

He stood next to Faith as they watched people pay money to throw pies—most missed, but the pie would splatter enough to get Connor messier with each toss. When one pie was left, Faith plunked down her money and stepped up to the line, the heavily whip-creamed pie in her hand.

"Please don't tell me you baked that one," Connor said. "I need something I can at least stand to lick off."

"Oh, you're going to pay for that."

Connor's grin only widened. Faith squared off, remembered all the tips Kaleb had given her when he taught her how to throw when she was a kid, and launched it, hitting him square in the face. She got even more cheers than Kaleb had.

Connor came out from behind the board. He wiped a hand over his face, shaking off a large portion of the pie, but it was still clinging to his eyelashes with smudges of white all over. He moved for her, and before she could react, he yanked her to him and kissed her. For a moment she tried to push away, but then she gave in, tasting whip cream and banana pudding as he kissed her.

With the event over, people sprung into action, using a hose to clean off the pie. One of the women from the committee offered Connor a washrag and he cleaned himself off as the festival wound down, all the work and magic coming to a close.

Kaleb put a hand on Faith's shoulder, glancing at Connor and then back at her, and she waited for another speech about how he didn't approve. "Just be careful, okay?"

Faith nodded. "Okay."

Connor approached, and another wordless conversation, like so many he and Kaleb seemed to have, passed between them. Then her brother gave her boyfriend a sort of half-salute, half-nod thing before walking away. Connor let out the same kind of exhale Kaleb had, all relief. She could tell he'd been upset things were off between them, and it looked like they were finally getting back on track.

A grin curved his lips as he drew her to him, sliding one of his hands under the back of her shirt. The lights from the gazebo cast a soft glow on his face, giving her a chance to soak in the stubble forming along his jaw, the slope of his nose, his perfect lips.

"I can only handle about another second of you looking at me like that before I do something about it," Connor said, digging his fingers into her skin and sending white-hot jabs of desire through her core.

She leaned closer so that her breasts pressed against his chest. "You think I'm scared?"

He peered into her eyes and suddenly she felt like she was naked, and not in a good way. "You are. But you shouldn't be."

Her heart beat against her rib cage. She licked her lips and Connor exhaled a shaky breath. She'd never felt so safe and out of control at the same time. "Take me home."

He swallowed, hard, and his voice came out husky. "Home, like...?"

"Yours."

. . .

The drive was torturously long, Faith sitting next to him in those blessedly tiny shorts, her hand high enough on his thigh to have him constantly readjusting in his seat, cursing the distance to his place.

She squeezed his thigh and shot him a naughty grin—she knew she was driving him crazy, and he was going to have to get her back for teasing him. He accelerated as his place came into sight. Just a few…more…seconds.

He turned into his driveway and killed the engine. In one fluid motion, he pulled Faith onto his lap, crushing his mouth to hers. He savored the familiar taste of her lips, her tongue. Faith ran her fingers through his hair and rocked her hips, making him groan. Fire built between them as they ran their fingers over each other's bodies and consumed each other's breaths.

Keeping his lips locked onto hers and his arm tight around her, he felt around for the truck's door handle. They stumbled toward his place, kissing and tugging on clothes. Faith peeled his shirt off in the living room. Hers hit the floor in the hall. Then her silky skin was against his bare chest, the thin lace of her bra the only thing between them. She slid her fingers in the waistband of his jeans and yanked him closer.

"I like it when you manhandle me," he said.

Faith undid the button of his jeans. "Then you're going to love what happens next."

Just when he didn't think he could get any more turned on, she said something like that. He lifted her into his arms, carried her into his room, and lowered her onto the bed. He slid off her shorts and paused to take her in, thinking he'd never seen anything so damn beautiful in his life.

Not only was she beautiful, she'd climbed under his skin and into his soul. For so long, he'd closed himself off to caring about someone, associating it with pain and disappointment. But his heart was wide open now, and it was scary and amazing, all at the same time. He felt like he should say something. Tell her that he cared about her. That she was the best thing that'd ever happened to him. Only he didn't know how to say it without it sounding like a line, and he didn't want to use lines with her.

Faith sat up and he pulled her to him. He kissed her long and deep, covered her body with his, and found that he didn't need any words after all.

. . .

Faith rested her head on Connor, thinking that there was nothing quite so comfortable as a guy's chest. Especially Connor's well-built, shirtless one. Her breaths were still coming faster than normal and every nerve ending in her body tingled. She'd expected the sex to be good, but there weren't even words to describe it. And the way he'd looked at her during—she'd never experienced that kind of intensity before.

He dragged his fingers up and down her back. After a moment, his hand stilled, and then he said, "My biggest fear in life used to be that I'd end up like my dad—that I'd get angry and hurt the people I claimed I loved. It was just easier to keep everyone at a safe distance…"

Faith twisted so she could see his face.

"I didn't mean to let you in, Faith. But I think you stole my heart that first night I laid eyes on you. I'd never hurt you. And I'd never let anyone else hurt you. I want you to know that."

A tight band formed around her lungs. She placed her hand over his heart, feeling it beating under his skin. "I know."

He relaxed, but his words reminded her who he was, making worry rise up and pick at her afterglow. When it came to hero complexes, his was above and beyond the norm. At first she'd thought he wanted recognition as a hero, but now she knew he was trying to save everyone because he didn't think he'd done enough when he was younger. She knew he'd sacrifice himself to help people, the same way her dad had.

"Baby? What is it?"

She shook her head. Going into it would ruin this perfect night, and she wanted to hold onto it a little longer. She scooted up, kissed his lips, and then wrapped herself around him, holding tight and telling herself they'd find a way to work it all out.

Chapter Sixteen

When Faith woke up, she could hear Connor talking to someone. He was pulling on his clothes, his phone pressed to his ear. Penny was pacing with him, her ears and eyebrows twitching with every movement Connor made.

"How bad?" Connor asked. There was silence and then his hand tightened around the phone. "A gun? Damn it to hell!" He gritted his teeth and shook his head. "Yeah, I'm coming. And when we go in, I hope that prick does pull a gun on me—I'd love an excuse."

A pit formed in Faith's stomach. She sat up, pulling the sheets up with her. Connor hung up the phone and glanced over. "Sorry, I didn't mean to wake you."

"Everything okay?" She held her breath, scared of what he'd say. Scared of what he wouldn't.

"I've got to go in to work. I don't know how long I'll be. But stay as long as you want, okay?" He leaned down and kissed her.

She grabbed his shirt, holding him there. "What's going on?"

"It's just work stuff. I'll call you later." He kissed her again, a way-too-short kiss, and then he was gone. Penny whimpered at the door, then came around the bed and jumped next to Faith. She whimpered again, and Faith felt like joining her. Her chest squeezed tighter and tighter as she ran her hand down the dog's back. Over and over she heard Connor say, *A gun?* and then, *I hope that prick does pull a gun on me.*

Control was slipping from her, her breaths were coming too fast, in and in but no out. All oxygen, no release.

Everywhere she looked, there was a reminder of who Connor was. A certificate declaring him an operator for the SWAT team. A picture of him being decorated next to a couple of other officers, most likely for dangerous acts of bravery.

She picked up her phone and called him, needing to hear his voice. Needing for him to tell her what was going on.

It rang and rang, and then his voice-mail message came on. His prerecorded voice didn't give her the reassurance she needed. She thought back to all the late nights Mom had spent pacing the floor, chewing her nails as she glanced at the clock. For every minute Dad was late, the thicker the tension hanging in the air got. The only thing worse than the pacing had been when it stopped.

A gun, a gun, a gun. Connor dealt with guns every day. Just like Dad had done.

Until the day his dangerous job had caught up to him.

When Faith squeezed her eyes closed, she saw Dad in his casket, Mom gripping the edge, tears running down her face. Icy shards of panic traveled through Faith's veins, turning everything inside her cold and hard.

"I can't do this," she whispered, bringing her trembling hands to her forehead. She wanted to be strong enough to be with Connor—wanted it so badly that she'd fooled herself into thinking it'd all work out somehow. In life, there were ways of coping with stressful situations, but you also needed to know yourself enough to learn how to avoid or remove yourself from circumstances that would put you in danger of panic attacks or dark holes of depression you might never crawl out of. If Connor got hurt—or worse—she'd never get over it. But if she tied her life to his permanently and it happened…

She couldn't survive it.

Not again.

Faith gathered her clothes, dressed as quickly as possible, and took one last glance around Connor's place.

Then she did what she did best.

She ran.

• • •

Kaleb glanced up when Faith charged through the front door. Ella was sitting next to him, eating Lucky Charms on the couch, even though food in the living room was supposedly a big no-no.

Her sorrow must've been written across her face because Kaleb stood. "Did he hurt you?"

Faith shook her head and tears pricked her eyes.

"He told you about how he knew Dad, didn't he?"

Faith sniffed. "Yeah. I mean, he told me the other day."

Kaleb stuck his hands in his pockets. "Well, I suppose that's it then. I worried he was going to hurt you, but when it comes down to it, he's a good guy. The best friend I've ever had, actually. Not many dudes, especially single dudes, would care to spend time with a guy, his wife, and kid. And if he told you about that, he's obviously serious about you."

Her throat grew so tight the ache traveled all the way down to her heart. "He is a good guy. But I don't think I can do it, Kaleb. Every time he leaves, I'll wonder if he's coming back. I tell myself over and over that it's a safe town, but then I see Dad in that casket and I..." A tear slipped down her cheek and she sniffed again. "Tell him I'm sorry. Tell him he deserves someone who can support him in who he is."

Kaleb's face dropped. "Faithie, don't do it. You can't keep running away."

She wiped the tears off her face with the back of her hand. "I'll be back. I just need a break. I've been meaning to visit Mom anyway. And I should travel around while I have the chance. Who knows when I'll get another break?" She glanced at Ella. "Can Mrs. Ferguson take her for a few days? If you can't find anyone else to watch her, of course I'll stay, but—"

"We can manage. Tell Mom we send our love and that we hope we'll see her after the baby comes." Kaleb put his hand on her shoulder and she could tell he was fighting his emotions, which only made her want to burst into tears. "We hope to see you, too."

Faith ran back to her bedroom and shoved the basics in a suitcase with as many clothes as she could. She knew this wasn't a healthy way to deal with things—that she was permanently messed up. Just another reason why she needed to get away before she ruined Connor's life as well as hers. Not to mention Kaleb's. It was long past time for him to have to take care of her whenever things went wrong.

Anna was asleep, so Faith pressed her hand to the door, wishing her a silent good-bye. Then she went into the living room and hugged Ella. Her niece wrapped her arms around her neck, and more tears escaped. "I love you, princess." She kissed Ella's cheek, then turned and hugged Kaleb. "I'm sorry. And don't forget to tell him I'm sorry."

It felt like her heart was ripping in two. If she stayed, though, she was afraid she might lose her heart—and herself—completely. For a while it would feel nice—being in Connor's arms, continuing to fall in love. But reality would creep in day by day and calls would always be coming in for him to go somewhere he might not come back from. She couldn't watch him do it, sick with worry all day every day.

So she'd get away for a while, find a spot close to campus right before her internship started—she'd even stay in a cheap motel if she had to—and start over again. Whenever she visited Cornelius, she'd avoid seeing Connor as much as possible. He'd get over it.

Probably much faster than she would.

• • •

Connor spent the day filing reports and contacting social workers, making sure that Erica would have a place to go as soon as she got out of the hospital—this time Hal had pulled a gun and threatened her with it in addition to beating her. As much as Connor wanted to arrest Hal, he'd let Sullivan do it. He'd been afraid he wouldn't be able to hold himself back from hitting the bastard, and he didn't want whatever lawyer Hal hired to be able to get him off because he couldn't hold his temper.

Aggravated battery was a serious offense, one he felt confident the prosecutor could get to stick with Erica's help. After personally escorting her to a friend's house, Connor drove to Kaleb's. He needed to see Faith. Needed to hold her in his arms and know that she was okay, so that he'd feel okay. He didn't see her car in the driveway, so he called her phone.

She didn't answer.

He walked up the sidewalk and knocked on the front door. As soon as Kaleb stepped onto the porch, Connor could tell something was wrong. He thought they'd had a breakthrough last night, but he was probably pissed at him for sleeping with Faith. Connor held up his hands. "I know, I know. But dude,

I swear I'll treat her right. I...I think I love her."

Kaleb let out a sigh. "Faith's gone."

Steel fingers wrapped around Connor's heart and lungs. "What do you mean she's gone?"

"I'm sorry, man. This is what she does. She told me to tell you she's sorry. Then she drove away, and I'm not sure when—or if—she'll be back."

. . .

Faith glanced at her phone. Connor. Again. She'd arrived in Wythesville several hours ago and was making up the tiny futon in the cramped office at her grandparents' so she'd have somewhere to sleep. They and Mom were thrilled she was there for a visit, which only made the lump of guilt in her stomach grow. Yes, she should've visited sooner, but she shouldn't have to flee to do it.

The phone rang again, and she couldn't take it anymore. He deserved a proper good-bye at least. The second she answered, Connor's deep voice filled her ear. "Blondie, you get your fine ass back here right now."

Faith gripped the phone, her knees shaking and her heart clenching so tight she couldn't breathe. "Look, you're a great guy and—"

"No, don't even start that. I'm not a great guy. I'm a pissed-off guy, and I'm about to trace your cell so I can come get you. I'll drag you back kicking and screaming if I have to."

All the air squeezed out of her lungs. "You're making this more difficult than it has to be."

"Good."

No matter how many times she tried to swallow, she couldn't. "I fooled myself into thinking I could get over the fact that you're a cop. That you're on that damned SWAT team. But I can't do it. It's just never going to work, Connor."

"I need you, Faith."

She blinked over and over, but the tears were coming faster than she could blink them back. Sure her legs were going to give out, she sat on the half-made futon. There were pictures in this room, ones of her parents with her and Kaleb, from so long ago, because there wasn't an option of taking complete family pictures after that. It only reiterated what she'd decided, but it didn't make this any easier.

"Do you know how hard it is for me to say that?" he asked.

"Do you know how hard it was for me to hear you talking about a gun this morning? How you *hoped* someone would try to take a shot at you? And then have you leave, not knowing if you were going to be okay? All I could think about was my dad. You put yourself in danger every day, and I can't do it. I care about you, more than I've ever cared about anyone else, but I can't do it." Her voice cracked and now she was full-on crying again.

She could hear his breaths on the other line and each one pierced her heart. Now she was sure she'd done the right thing. If he were standing in front of her, she'd never be able to break it off. "You really are a hero. You're amazing." Tears blurred her vision and pain radiated out from her chest. "But I can't be with you. I'm so sorry."

Before he could try to argue, she disconnected the call and tossed the phone away.

Chapter Seventeen

Connor couldn't remember the last time he'd felt so irritated at everything. His morning run had revved him up instead of calming him, and on the way to work, he'd wanted to ram his truck into cars going too slow—probably unprofessional for a cop. And now he was seconds away from chucking the empty coffeepot across the room.

How hard was it to start a new batch? He imagined the satisfaction the shattering glass would give him. For a moment.

Then it'd be Faith, Faith, Faith, all over again. He rubbed his hands over his face. It'd been six long days and he was still furious at her for leaving. Last night he'd nearly gone to the Rusty Anchor to find a girl to take home—any girl to help erase the memories of Faith, the scent of her lingering on the pillowcase she'd slept on. Only he knew no one else could erase how it felt to be with Faith, and the fact of the matter was, he didn't want to erase her. And that pissed him off even more.

All the years controlling his temper, keeping himself in

check, guarding his emotions, and one tiny blonde unraveled everything. The emptiness was back, but worse, because now he knew what it was like to have it gone. Then he'd get angry all over again and feel like a failure, because he liked it better than the sadness, and it made him see why his dad chose it.

He slammed the coffeepot back down without bothering to refill it and headed back to his desk and the stack of never-ending paperwork. He didn't want to be stuck inside the office. He needed to be out on patrol with enough things going on that he could stop thinking about Faith.

She'd told him he was a hero, but that she couldn't be with him. Basically that was the reason she *wouldn't* be with him.

He picked up a pen and tapped it against the desk. Could he do something else? There was security work—she'd probably still think that was too dangerous. He'd fought the urge to call her and tell her—or her voice mail, since she refused to pick up—that she was being ridiculously stubborn. Everything in life was a risk. It was more of a risk to not have well-trained cops on the streets.

He tossed his pen across his desk and swore.

"You okay over there?" Kaleb asked, glancing around his computer monitor.

"Your sister pisses me off."

"I told you it was a bad idea. But if it makes you feel any better, I talked to her yesterday and she sounds miserable."

It does, he immediately thought, but then the thought of her miserable made his chest ache. Seriously, he was such a mess. He turned to his computer and started inputting data. He was good at math. He supposed he could look into a career in that field.

He'd hate it, though.

No, screw that. He wasn't changing his career for a girl who'd just run if things got too hard. He'd live his life the way he wanted. Eventually the hollowness would go away.

If he told himself that enough times, maybe one day it'd be true.

· · ·

For weeks Faith had wanted to sleep in. Wanted peace and quiet and a day of nothing stretched before her. But she found that she hated it. There was no pitter-patter of little feet to wake her up. No Ella climbing in her bed to hug her or ask for chocolate milk or nail polish. No sexy cop waking her with a kiss, *Sleeping Beauty* style.

Instead of getting better, the spot between her ribs ached deeper by the day. Telling herself she'd be okay if she forced herself into motion, she threw on running gear and headed outside. It wasn't a bad running path, but it wasn't as beautiful as running along glittering Lake Norman.

Connor had probably completed his run with Penny hours ago. Her feet faltered and she shook her head. Space was supposed to help her forget about Connor, not make it impossible to think about anything else. When she'd moved before or cut someone out of her life, she'd had the occasional thought of the past or who she'd left behind, but it wasn't all-consuming like this, where she could feel every mile of space between her and where she'd left.

By the time she got back to the house, Mom had already made and cleaned up breakfast. Grandma and Grandpa were in their recliners. *The Price is Right* blared at an ear-shattering level from the TV, but Grandpa was somehow sleeping through it, already on his first nap of the day.

Grandma smiled up at her. "Morning, honey."

Faith leaned down and hugged her. "Morning. Need anything?"

She shook her head and turned her attention back to

the TV. Faith took a quick shower, grabbed a mug of coffee, and stepped outside, where Mom was working in the garden. Mom sat back and swiped her arm across her forehead. Mud covered her gloves and the knees of her clothes, but she looked happy there in the dirt.

"Can you bring me that watering can?" Mom asked.

Faith set down her mug on the patio table and grabbed the plastic watering can. She knelt down in the dirt and tugged at the weeds, figuring she might as well help.

"Are you ever going to tell me why you really showed up?" Mom asked, and Faith paused midpull. When Faith was a little girl, Mom used to have a sixth sense that she was sad or having a hard time. But after Dad died, it seemed like she didn't notice anything. Staring at her now, Faith saw more of the mother who'd raised her than she had in years.

That was all it took for the whole story to burst out of her. She started at when she was eighteen, how she'd needed to get away from Cornelius as soon as she could—something Mom could relate to—to how she'd run when her ex had cheated on her, up to how she'd realized she was falling for Connor, got scared, and drove to Virginia to escape.

Mom sucked in a deep breath and blew it out. "I was hoping you'd figured out how to deal with the past better than I did."

Faith shook her head. "I took classes and read through studies and…I still haven't figured it out. I mean, I think I made peace with it, though I'll never stop missing Daddy. But to knowingly go into a relationship with a man who faces the same dangers? To live my life the way you had to? How did you do it?"

Mom set down her spade and pressed her lips together. "I loved your father since I was sixteen years old. It's true that I didn't realize what I was getting into, being the wife of a cop. But if I could go back and change the past, I'd still marry him." Her voice quivered and her eyes glistened with unshed tears. "Even though part of me died with him."

Faith reached out and took Mom's hand.

"I've found joy again, though." She gestured around the garden. "My plants, helping my parents. You, Kaleb, Anna, and little Ella. You guys make me happy. All of it keeps me going."

"But you still haven't been back to Cornelius since you left."

Mom gave her a sad smile. "I have been rather good at avoiding going back, making your brother drag his family out here instead of traveling to North Carolina. I've been talking with a counselor again, and I'm planning on going when Anna has that baby. It's time. It's beyond time."

"I'll help you," Faith said. Of course that meant she'd have to go back, too. She heard Connor's voice again, the way she had for the past several days. *I need you.* Every time, the words dug deeper into her heart until it felt like it was constantly bleeding. She put her hand on her chest, pushing against the pain. She'd never felt this badly about a breakup, not even with guys she'd been with for months.

This is ridiculous. I barely know him.

But immediately she knew that wasn't true. She thought of how he'd taken her to meet his family and then let her in on a past she could tell he didn't share with anyone. Then she was picturing him as a kid, afraid of his dad but calling the police to keep his mom safe. He'd helped her face her fears and let her in. And she'd left him.

"I screwed everything up, Mom. I thought I could run away from Connor before I fell too hard—that it'd be better for us both in the end. But it's too late. I want him in my life. I *need* him in my life." Everything inside her felt like it was coming apart. "I'm in love with him."

In love. With a hero. The one thing she'd sworn to never

let herself do. "And I just left him. And Kaleb and Anna, after everything they've done for me." Faith stood and brushed the dirt from her knees. "I can't keep running. I need to be stronger than this."

Mom stood, too. "Don't beat yourself up. It's not easy. But you've got a good heart. And you are strong." She hugged Faith tightly, as if she wanted to squeeze years of missed-out-on hugs all into this one.

When they headed back into the house, *The Price is Right* was no longer blaring, a breaking-news alert on-screen instead.

The bank in Mooresville flashed on the screen, and the reporter was saying something about a hostage situation. Faith dropped her mug, the last of her coffee spilling on the pale wooden floor.

"They'll call in Kaleb and Connor," she said, though it didn't seem like it'd come from her lips. The world spun, and she was afraid to move. Blink. Breathe. Darkness pressed in on her and her lungs stopped working.

Mom put her hand on Faith's shoulder.

Faith didn't want to worry her, but she knew it was true. Their SWAT unit was the closest to the bank. If anything happened, and she didn't get the chance to tell Connor how she felt, she'd never forgive herself.

"I've gotta go."

. . .

"We just got the call," Connor said, lowering the phone and looking at Kaleb. He'd done the SWAT training, wanting to be prepared, and even considered transferring to Charlotte so he'd be able to use his skills to help more people. But part of him thought it'd never actually happen.

"The call? You mean…?"

"Three shooters went into the bank up in Mooresville. Apparently they're holding hostages. Grab your gear; we've gotta go."

Adrenaline pumped through Connor's veins as they rushed out of the station. He was already mentally preparing himself, going over everything he'd learned in his head. At the door to the car, he hesitated and glanced at Kaleb. "You've got your family to think about. If you want to sit this one—"

"Don't even finish that. We're going to go take out the bad guys. End of story."

"Damn straight." Connor got into the car, flipped on the lights, and sped toward Mooresville, where they'd gather the team and come up with a plan.

The drive flew by and then they were covered in SWAT gear, grabbing rifles, and listening as the plan was detailed and they were all assigned tasks for if the negotiations fell through. Waiting took forever, each second an eternity while covered in gear, ready to spring into action if necessary. The situation escalated as negotiations went sour, and they were concerned human lives were at risk if they didn't act. The three shooters were in one area, away from the hostages, and they weren't sure they'd get another chance. So the captain gave the go signal.

Connor held the butt of his rifle tight to his shoulder, swinging as he scanned the area. Even though it was their first mission, everyone was moving smoothly, as if they'd done it a dozen times before.

The call to fire went through the earpieces. Shots rang out. The first shooter went down. Then the second.

Gunfire erupted behind them. Apparently the third guy had circled around. Connor turned. Through the dim lights he spotted the third guy, and the barrel of his gun was aimed at Kaleb. Time ground to a halt, yet spun too fast. Faith's image flashed before his eyes. He thought of Anna and Ella.

Then he dove onto his partner.

The bullet hit his back, a thousand fists to his spine all at once. He rolled, pulled his pistol, and shot the guy, three in the chest. Eerie, ringing silence followed.

Each breath hurt and no matter how many Connor took, he couldn't get any oxygen. Cold sweat pricked his forehead. He tried to push up, but the floor came at him instead. He could hear Kaleb yelling but couldn't make out the words. As he let his eyes drift closed, he thought that at least Faith wouldn't have to go through losing another family member.

· · ·

None of the damn radio stations were giving Faith any information on the hostage situation. Daddy had often lectured about speeding, and she'd always remained in the limits at all times. But as she whizzed toward Mooresville, she pushed her vehicle to the limit, driving as fast as she dared.

She wanted to call Mom, but knew it'd only make her anxiety go crazy, and same with Anna. It was too risky, especially with her pregnancy. So she kept driving, fighting off panic attacks of her own. She couldn't stop thinking of the day two officers had shown up at her home. Mom fell to her knees, screaming *no* over and over again. Kaleb went to pick her up and see what had happened. Then he'd come over, took both of Faith's hands in his, and told her Daddy was gone.

It had seemed so unreal—Daddy could take on anything. She kept thinking he'd walk in through the front door and it'd all be a bad dream. But with every hour, reality sank in. Reality came faster now than it had then, a slap in the face, screaming in her ears.

Tears burned her eyes and a giant lump formed in her throat. She wanted to pull over and cry—wanted to curl into a ball and never have to face reality again. But she had to get to Connor and her brother. Summoning all the strength she had, she gripped the wheel tighter and turned onto the road that would take her into Mooresville.

Traffic grew thicker and thicker as she entered the town, the vehicles around her slowing to a crawl. Brake lights permanently glowed in front of her, her nerves stretched tighter and tighter, and her morbid imagination got worse and worse. If they'd blocked off the roads, that meant it was as dangerous as she'd feared.

Faith swallowed and told herself to remain calm. It didn't really work, what with the fact her rapid pulse was thundering through her head and her stomach wouldn't stop churning. Finally, the outline of the bank and the lights of at least a half-dozen cop cars came into view. Only that made traffic even worse.

"Come on, come on." Didn't people know that two of the people she loved most in the world were up there? That they might need her?

Unless I'm too late. Faith shook her head. *No thinking like that.* After five minutes of being gridlocked, she abandoned her car. Other drivers yelled and honked, but she didn't care. She sprinted toward the police line, focused on the red-and-blue lights.

An officer she didn't recognize stepped in front of her when she reached the blockade. "Ma'am! You have to stay back!"

"I'm looking for Kaleb Fitzpatrick and Connor Maguire. They're on the SWAT team, and I need to know if they're okay."

"Sorry, ma'am, I don't have that information. You'll have to stay back."

She waited until he'd turned to someone else, ducked under the barrier, and ran toward the bank. Two arms wrapped around her and jerked her back—the same officer. She turned and started crying and yelling and begging, but he just kept repeating his earlier instructions.

She gripped the guy's shirt. "I know you don't know me, but please, please see if you can find out about Officers Fitzpatrick and Maguire. Please!"

Another officer approached, and she recognized the Cornelius Sherriff Department logo on his shirt. His name tag said he was Officer Johnson. "Did you say Fitzpatrick and Maguire?" he asked.

Her heart practically leaped out of her chest. "Yes! Do you know how they are?"

Officer Johnson glanced toward the entrance of the bank, where there were more cops, cop cars, and a giant SWAT vehicle. His gaze came back to her. "You're Kaleb's little sister, right?"

She nodded frantically.

"And Maguire's girl."

Pain twisted her heart—she hoped she was still his girl. "Yes, that's me. Please, I need to know what's going on."

"I've got it from here," he said, pulling her to the side so Officer Anal could go work the barrier again. "The team charged in and took out the first two shooters, but the third one got a shot off."

Faith grabbed onto Officer Johnson's arm to keep from falling to the ground. Fear had her in a vise grip and it was squeezing tighter and tighter, making it hard to breathe, move, speak.

"The shot was aimed at Fitzpatrick," Officer Johnson continued, "but he's okay. Maguire… He pushed Fitzpatrick out of the way and took the hit. But he still managed to take out the shooter."

A fresh wave of tears burned Faith's eyes. It was too much like Daddy, and she was terrified to ask, but she had to know. She licked her dry lips. "Is he...?"

"All I know is that they took him to Lake Norman Regional."

She tightened her grip on Officer Johnson's arm. "My vehicle's stuck back on the road with all the traffic, and I need to get to the hospital now." He looked like he was going to say he couldn't take her, so she locked eyes with him and said, "Please. I never even told him I loved him, and if something happens to him... Just *please*."

Officer Johnson sighed, then pulled her toward a squad car.

• • •

Connor kept insisting he was fine, pushing away all the nurses with their blood-pressure cuffs and lights to look into and pulse checks. The bulletproof vest was a level three, able to stop handguns and high-powered rifles—he had proof it worked, though it definitely hadn't felt good when the bullet hit him. Hurt like a bitch, actually. But having people check his vitals every two seconds didn't make any of his injuries feel any better. Finally they'd left him alone for two seconds. As soon as he saw Faith enter the room, though, he decided he'd hit his head harder than he thought. Now he was hallucinating. As far as hallucinations went, at least this one was nice to look at.

Her bottom lip quivered, and then she burst into tears. "You're alive. They told me you were, but I..." She put both hands over her heart.

He blinked, still processing her sudden appearance in his room.

"What the hell were you thinking, jumping in front of a bullet like that?"

That was the moment he knew she wasn't a hallucination.

Only Faith would yell at him while he was in a hospital bed, his back and side aching so badly it hurt to breathe.

He'd thought he'd be mad the next time he saw her—had a whole angry speech planned and everything. But as she wiped at the tears running down her cheeks, everything inside him turned to mush. All he wanted was her closer.

Daggers of white-hot pain shot through his spine as he reached out for her. He jerked back his arm and tried to cover his wince. "Come 'ere."

She lunged, throwing her arms around him and burying her head in his neck, her tears wet against his skin. He wrapped his right arm—the one that didn't cause as much pain—around her. Physically, it still ached to hold her, but inside, the heaviness he'd carried around since she'd left evaporated. Pleasure and pain. The perfect description for this girl.

"I suppose now wouldn't be the best time to make a case for how safe my job is?" His attempt to lighten the mood was met with more tears and Faith tightening her hold on him. He kissed the top of her head. "It's nothing, baby. Just a few bruises." He decided to leave out the fractured-ribs part. "I'll be on my feet in a couple hours."

She sat up and drew her eyebrows together in what was probably supposed to be a stern expression but only came across as adorable. "No, you will not. I'm coming with you to your house, and you're going to sit back while I take care of you."

That sent all sorts of dirty images through his head. He reached up and wound a strand of her silky hair around his finger. "Are you going to wear a sexy-nurse outfit?"

"I'd smack you if you weren't already beat-up." She shook her head and then leaned down and pressed her mouth to his. Again, and again, kiss after delicious kiss, but they were never quite long enough. "You're not invincible, you know."

Another kiss. "Why'd you do that?" She pulled back and regarded him, obviously wanting a serious answer.

"Your brother's my best friend. And"—he glanced at the beeping monitor and then brought his gaze back to her—"I thought of you, and how heartbroken you'd be if anything happened to him."

She pressed her lips together and it looked like she might start crying again. "I'd be heartbroken if something happened to you, too, you idiot."

Warmth flooded his chest. "So you're saying you care about me a little bit?"

She ran her hand down his cheek and brushed her fingertips across his jaw, making his heart jerk in his chest. "I'm afraid I'm kind of in love with you." The warmth spread, filling every inch of him and making his head buzz.

"And all I had to do was take a bullet to finally get that confession," he said. She gently nudged him and he yanked her to him, until her chest was against his and he had better access to her lips. He took his time kissing her, soaking in every tiny moan and the taste of her mouth, wishing he wasn't wearing this damn hospital gown. Then he peered into her big green eyes and said, "I love you, too, Blondie. Don't ever leave me again."

"I won't, I swear. I'm sorry. It's just that I wasn't supposed to fall for a hero. I tried so hard not to..." She ran her fingers through his hair, sending tingly zips across his scalp and then traced his lips with her thumb, as if she was memorizing them. "But I failed. Like epically failed. I can't help but worry about you and your job, but I decided that it's easier to be with you and worry than not be with you at all."

He pressed his hand to the small of her back and wrapped his fingers around her side. "You don't have to worry, babe." He raised an eyebrow and shot her a smile. "As you can see, I'm clearly a badass."

She curled her hand around the back of his neck and stuck her forehead against his. "But you're *my* badass."

"Damn straight." He kissed her again, the sensation of her lips, her tongue twisting with his, better than any painkiller.

Of course the nurse chose that moment to come in to get more vitals. He was slightly irritated still—his vitals were clearly working just fine—but with Faith's hand in his, he figured he could deal with it. As long as she was with him, he could deal with whatever came at him.

Chapter Eighteen

Faith glanced over at Connor. He looked even bigger in her car, his legs and arms and massive body barely fitting in the tiny space. A blindfold covered his eyes. "No peeking."

"I'm digging this kinky side of you, Faith Fitzpatrick."

Faith shook her head and pulled up in front of the Rusty Anchor. She quickly got out of the car and helped Connor. "Okay, watch the step."

He lifted his foot much higher than the sidewalk, but that was better than tripping, at least. After five days, he was finally moving better and the giant bruise on the left side of his back that'd been black and blue was fading to purple and yellow.

Keeping one hand on his elbow, Faith pushed open the door to the Rusty Anchor.

Cheers erupted and Faith reached onto her toes and took off the blindfold so he could see the guys from the station and the rest of the SWAT team, Dani, Wes, Brynn, Sawyer, Paul, and Carly, along with Connor's entire family and Anna, Kaleb, and Ella. She'd wanted to do something big. As the smile spread across his face, happiness bubbled up in her, too.

He leaned down and kissed her cheek. "Thanks, babe," he said and then moved into the crowd, getting lots of guy-hugs and slaps that made her flinch for him. *Watch his back and ribs,* she silently aimed toward them, though Connor didn't seem to notice. All the guys in black, the Rusty Anchor—it was a lot like the first night she'd laid eyes on Connor Maguire. Except she wasn't angry anymore. She wasn't even fighting her ghosts. Every day things got better.

She was living in Cornelius again and dating a cop, two things she'd sworn she'd never do—there really was something to that never say never saying.

Ella ran through the crowd, a pink princess in a sea of dark colors. She ran to Connor first, who tossed her in the air—dang guy never took it easy like he was supposed to. Ella leaned for Faith, and she carried her as she and Connor moved around the room, talking with his family and the guys he worked with.

After a while, Faith split off to the table where Anna and Kaleb were seated. Ella lunged for Kaleb and he let her stand on his lap. Faith glanced at Anna. "How are you feeling?"

"It's so good to be out. Exhausting, but nice." Anna put her hand on her stomach. "And I haven't had any contractions so far, but it's a relief to know that we're in the safe zone now if it does happen."

"Holy shit," Kaleb said, his eyes on the door.

"Shit!" Ella parroted and Anna frowned and said, "Kaleb!"

But when Faith turned, she had the same thought. She'd invited Mom, but didn't think she'd actually come. Mom, in Cornelius. Not just Cornelius, either. The Rusty Anchor—Daddy's place. Pride welled up in Faith, along with the urge to burst into tears. She ran over and hugged her, squeezing her the way she'd squeezed Faith back in Virginia. Trying to silently tell her that she was here for her if she needed help coping with all the memories. Kaleb and Ella joined in on the hugging, and Anna wasn't far behind.

Connor came over and put his hand on Faith's back. "Connor," Faith said, "this is my mom, Mary Fitzpatrick. Mom, Connor."

Connor shook Mom's hand. "It's an honor to meet you."

"Thank you." She placed her other hand over their clasped ones. "So, you're the guy."

Connor flashed his killer grin at Faith and then nodded at Mom. "I'm the guy."

There were more introductions, food, music, and drinks. Faith was over at the bar getting a refill when her gaze drifted to Dad's picture. Her heart tugged, like it always did, but there was happiness protecting it from letting the sorrow take over.

Connor came up behind her, wrapped his arms around her, and kissed her cheek. Daddy was Connor's hero, and he'd always be hers as well. But her brother and the guy holding her now were her heroes, too. She knew she was going to have to be strong as she dealt with the stress of worrying about them and being involved with a man who spent long hours on a job that never quite ended. But she knew she could do it—that she was going to have to be a different kind of hero. She might not be able to take out bad guys, but she could be a comforting shoulder, a listening ear, and a counselor to those who did. For Connor, she could be a soft place for him to fall at the end of the day, and loving him would give her the strength she'd need to be there for him.

She stared at Dad's smiling image, and she knew he'd be proud of how all his kids turned out, including the little boy who used to call him for help.

She grabbed the two Cokes—Connor was still taking pain pills, and she was driving—and turned to face her sexy cop, handing him one of them. He took a large swig, set his glass on the bar, then hooked a finger through her belt loop and tugged her close. "So I decided that I'm leaving the bar with a hot blonde tonight."

Faith raised an eyebrow. "Oh yeah?"

"Yeah." He took her glass from her and pressed his body against hers, leaving no doubt where his thoughts were headed. Heat flared between them and she bit her lip. His hungry eyes followed the gesture and he made a low noise in the back of his throat.

She leaned in and brushed her lips against his, pulling back when he tried to kiss her. He growled and another wave of heat shot through her core. In the next instant, she was in his arms. "Connor, put me down. You're going to hurt your back, and your ribs aren't healed yet."

"My back's just fine. And I'm ready to go home." He nodded at the crowd as he walked through. A bunch of guys whooped and hollered and Faith's cheeks burned with embarrassment.

She sighed. "You're such a caveman sometimes."

Connor shot her a crooked grin, tightening his grip on her. "How else am I supposed to let everyone know you're mine?" He pushed out of the restaurant. The sun had set, and like that night when she'd first started to think there was more to Connor, lightning bugs glittered all around them, out in full force tonight.

The rest of the world disappeared, and it was just Connor holding her in his massive arms, staring down at her with such affection she thought her heart might burst. "You're the best thing that ever happened to me," he said.

Faith put her hand on his cheek, running her palm down the scruff he'd let grow the past few days, and gently pressed her lips to his. Then she did her best cocky Connor impression. "Right back at you, babe."

Epilogue

Connor glanced around the decked-out atrium of the Levine Museum. At first he'd thought Wes was kidding when he said he was getting married in a museum. He'd never expected the large room with flowers and tables and twinkling lights.

He tugged on his tie and then held up the boutonniere Wes's mom had just given him. The tux he could rock, but a rose with tiny flowers bursting from it?

"Right?" Wes asked, holding up his own boutonniere. "Dani said she didn't care if we had them, but my mom and sisters said *everyone* would notice, and you couldn't just not have them."

"Come on, guys," Faith said. "Where's your sense of adventure? You can jump out of a helicopter but you can't handle wearing a little flower on your lapel?" She took the boutonniere out of Connor's hand and pinned it on for him.

He didn't get weddings, but he now got wanting to spend your entire life with someone. The past three months with Faith had been amazing, whether they were chilling at home or doing adventure tours with Dani and Wes. When Faith had gotten serious about apartment hunting in Charlotte again, what with her internship starting, Connor found he didn't like the thought of her living a town away. So he'd asked her to move in with him instead, and luckily, she'd said yes. He liked that she fussed over him, like now, when she was fixing his collar and running her hands down his tux to make sure it was all in order. She still couldn't cook for shit, so they ate a lot of takeout, or he grilled. He was happier than he'd ever been, and he'd do anything for the feisty blonde in front of him—he didn't even care if that made him whipped.

Nate Walsh, Wes's cousin who'd gone to the police academy with Connor, walked over to them. He was holding hands with a pretty blonde who had purple-and-blue streaks through her hair and tattoos peeking out of her strappy dress.

Connor shook Nate's hand and pulled him in for a one-armed hug. "How you been, man?"

"Good." Nate glanced at the girl at his side, and she grinned at him. "Awesome, actually." After he'd graduated the police academy, he'd gone back to his small hometown near the mountains to be a cop there.

"Looks like that helicopter ride was worth it," Wes said, smiling at Nate and his girlfriend, and Connor remembered he'd mentioned flying to Marion and then Kentucky on New Year's Eve to help Nate try to win over a girl. Apparently, it'd worked.

Nate introduced Kelsey to them, Connor introduced Faith, and then Wes's mom came over and asked them to all take their places. They walked down the aisle like they'd practiced the night before. Connor was paired with Brynn. He and Faith had gone out fishing with her, Sawyer, Anna, and Kaleb last weekend. It'd been Anna's first outing since having Patrick Connor Fitzpatrick. Ella was crazy about her new little brother, even though he didn't do much besides cry and sleep.

As crazy as it was hanging with Kaleb and his family right now, Connor couldn't help thinking about the day he and Faith would have kids of their own. He caught her eye in the crowd and winked at her. After they'd lined up at the front, the "Wedding March" started and Dani came down the aisle.

Wes's face lit up with a lovesick grin Connor might've given him a bad time about a few months ago. But now he got it. He glanced at Faith again, a thrill going through his gut when she was looking back at him, a beautiful smile on her face. He'd had his doubts about love before, but there was no doubt anymore.

She raised an eyebrow, eyes full of mischief, and his blood heated. He couldn't believe she could still drive him so crazy with a simple glance. He had a feeling that one day in the not so distant future, he'd be asking Kaleb for his blessing.

He was even pretty sure that his best friend would give it to him.

Acknowledgments

There are always so many people to thank, and different people help me every book. (Some of the same people help me through it as well.) And oh my gosh, I wrote a whole series! Now that I'm thinking about how it's the end of the Accidentally in Love series, I'm getting a little misty. It's just been so much fun! Thanks to Stacy Abrams once again for asking me if I wanted to write for the Bliss line—totally changed my life. Thanks for pushing me to be better even when I don't know how I'm gonna pull it off, and for your insight. Same to Alycia Tornetta. I'm so glad to have you both on my team. Thanks to Heather Riccio, publicist ninja who's helped me out a ton throughout the past couple of years. Jessica Turner and Debbie Suzuki, thanks for all of your help as well! I get to work with so many awesome people! Everyone at Entangled has been so great, from the editors to publicists to the other authors I'm so proud to be associated with. Thanks to Rachel Harris for the brainstorming sessions, as well as Brandy Vallance and Evangeline Denmark, who got the first glimpse at Connor and always make writing more fun. Lisa Burstein and Ophelia London, you both rock and help keep me sane—so glad I know you! Also, thanks to Victoria James for the help with the Italian in this book.

Huge shout-out to Jess Anderson, who answered all of my SWAT questions and gave me cool acronyms and terms to use. I'm super-impressed by what you do (and even more impressed because you take care of my awesome aunt Malinda.) Malinda, thanks for always being one of my biggest cheerleaders, and for knowing one day outside of Taco Bell, that I'd make it. LOL. Thanks to Nichole Vikdal for all of the info on pottery. That was much needed when I was looking for an extra something to add, and I'm also awed by your talent.

As always, thanks to my family—my parents, brothers and sisters, awesome kids, and my husband, Michael. Also to my friend Amanda Price, for keeping me entertained as I write and making me laugh when I have a bad day. Shout out to the TZWNDU Book Club! Love you gals! I've met so many awesome book bloggers, and I'm grateful for each one of you for help spreading the word about my books and for the reviews. I always worry about leaving someone out, but I've got to give an extra shout-out to Autumn, Andrea, Karen, and Monique.

And last, but certainly not least, is all of my readers! You guys rock, and this past year I've had so many dreams come true because of you! THANKS!

About the Author

Cindi Madsen is a *USA Today* bestselling author of contemporary romance and young adult novels. She sits at her computer every chance she gets, plotting, revising, and falling in love with her characters. Sometimes it makes her a crazy person. Without it, she'd be even crazier. She has way too many shoes, but can always find a reason to buy a pretty new pair, especially if they're sparkly, colorful, or super tall. She loves music and dancing and wishes summer lasted all year long. She lives in Colorado (where summer is most definitely NOT all year long) with her husband, three children, an overly-dramatic tomcat, & an adorable one-eyed kitty named Agent Fury.

You can visit Cindi at: www.cindimadsen.com, where you can sign up for her newsletter to get all the up-to-date information on her books.

Follow her on Twitter @cindimadsen.

Find your Bliss with these great releases…

THE DOCTOR'S FAKE FIANCÉE
a *Red River* novel by Victoria James

Former surgeon and bachelor Evan Manning has one thing on his mind—to reclaim the career that a car accident stole from him. But when he's forced to return to his hometown of Red River, Evan comes face-to-face with the gorgeous woman who's haunted his dreams for the last year—the woman he rescued from the burning car that injured his hand. When artist Grace Matheson's sexy hero hears that she needs work, he offers her a job and a home—if she'll pretend she's his fiancée for a month. The more time they spend together, the more real their feelings become—and the more likely heartbreak is.

HOW TO LOSE A BACHELOR
a novel by Anna Banks

Revenge has never been so fun… Rochelle Ransom has big plans for winning the prize money on a dating show to help her favorite charity—and if she wins the hot bachelor's heart, even better. But at the last minute she finds out the bachelor is her ex-boyfriend, Grant Drake. Now she's determined to get herself voted off as quickly as possible—even if she has to embarrass herself on national television. But Grant has a different plan for the woman who stole his heart.

HATE TO LOVE HIM
a *Kendrick Place* novel by Jody Holford

Whenever Brady Davis and Mia Kendrick are in the same room, sparks fly—both the bad and good kind. Brady's worried Mia's focus on big business could be the end of the tight-knit community he's created at Kendrick Place, while Mia can't ever let another man stand in the way of her dreams. Brady could have the power to change her mind…if he can get inside her heart.

Made in the USA
Middletown, DE
20 August 2020